<u>Only The Dead:</u>

<u>An African War</u>

<u>By</u>

<u>M.W.Duncan</u>

Preface

Hello readers. You're about to embark on a tale set during the turmoil of the second Liberian Civil War. For those of you familiar with this time and part of the world you may notice that I have altered the course of the war slightly. I did this to allow myself a fresh location to write in. For those of you who don't know about the conflict, I urge you to investigate and read some books or articles about this horrific and bloody period of history.

This novella would not have been completed without the help of several people. Without you all, this would probably have languished as an incomplete piece. Stephanie, Kirkus, Danielle, Pauline, Lynn, Nicola, Stew, Rebecca, Jane, Rachael and all others who have supported, encouraged and helped, thank you.

An African War is the first of several novellas in the Only The Dead series. I hope you all enjoy the story as much as I enjoyed writing it. For those who wish to find me on the web you can follow me on these sites. Until next time.

www.facebook.com/mwduncanwriter

https://twitter.com/MarkWDuncan

http://mwduncan.wordpress.com/

Chapter One

The heat created a dancing mirage on the road before me, a twisting of my vision, there for a moment before disappearing. I wiped at the sweat on my brow, and swatted insects away. It was a fact of Africa. It was a fact of Liberia. There were flies, and worse. Twice since arriving in Zorzor, I'd seen scorpions scuttling through the town, once even over my boots. Small, delicate almost, but with deadly stingers.

I stepped off the porch of the manor house, a building that wouldn't have looked out of place on a turn-of-the-century plantation in southern America. It was the grandest structure in Zorzor, made of a reddish brick and wood. The once-white paint now clung scantily, peeling, reducing the building to a poor mockery of what it once must have looked like. Most of the buildings were crude huts with corrugated iron coverings for roofs. I slung my AK-47 over my shoulder and stepped out onto the dirt road. Shell casings were thick on the ground. They crunched and clinked underfoot like pebbles on the beach.

Dropped in the middle of the jungle, this island of calm was restive compared to many regions of Liberia. Zorzor was still, stagnant, and full of soldiers, only no battle was being fought. At least, not yet. I was with LURD rebels, Liberians United for Reconciliation and Democracy, fighting the corrupt government of President Charles Taylor. Described by many as the worst tyrant West Africa had seen, he clung to power and a fictional legitimacy. His forces controlled less than half the country.

In the distance, I heard vehicles, and hoped it was the new batch of recruits and ammunition I was expecting. I walked through the town. Several fighters called out greetings as I passed. "Mak, Mak." No one seemed to pronounce my name properly. Mak had stuck. I gave them a rough salute, which they returned with a cheer.

I arrived at the edge of town and watched the road stretch back into the jungle, back to LURD-controlled territory. Three Toyota pickups kicked up dust as they headed toward Zorzor. Some of the rebels saw them, chanting and waving their AKs in celebration. The din caused a small crowd to gather around me as they welcomed the new recruits.

I watched in silence as the convoy pulled into town. A few of the younger fighters sang, their voices combining in a euphoric chorus. The recruits jumped down off the vehicles and I tried to ignore how many of them appeared to be on the wrong side of puberty. Many, boys plucked from other villages at the point of a gun. The commander of the forces in Zorzor, Tiger King, waved me over. He smiled, showing off impossibly white teeth.

"You see, Mak, we 'av 'nough ammo now."

I gave him an agreeing smile and went to inspect the supplies. We had been promised ten thousand rounds for the AKs and at least fifty new RPG rockets. When I moved between the trucks, it became clear there couldn't have been more than half that number delivered.

"Fuck me," I muttered, picking up a couple of extra magazines and stuffing them into my pockets. If the rebels' goal was to move on the capital, then they would have to sort out their supply issues.

It was a poorly guarded secret that the government of Guinea, eager to see the war-mongering Taylor ousted without getting their hands dirty, was trickling supplies to the rebels. Guinea's government would have to increase the amount of support if LURD were to make any headway. If I knew it stuck in the back of beyond, LURD hierarchy must know it back in Voinjama.

"Hey! Hey you!"

Clear spoken English? In Zorzor? I turned and found a white male running toward me with a small camera in his hand. He wore a beige photographer's vest, loaded with equipment. As he drew nearer it was clear he was new to Liberia. His vest did little to hide the paunch beneath, his lips weren't cracked, and his pale skin remained unburned by the sun.

"Hey," he said, out of breath. "You speak English? American?"

I paused a moment before replying, "I speak English. I'm British."

He threw out a hand. "Great, that's perfect. Should have known from the accent. Sorry, I'm Kyle Grant."

"Reporter?"

"Video journalist. I'm here to document the war, the people fighting it and the effects on the nation."

His explanation sounded rehearsed, one used to impress important people. I nodded at him. "Happy for you. Enjoy your stay in Liberia." I turned back toward the manor house.

"Wait, I would love to ask you a few questions. Would you be up for a little interview?"

"Do me a favour and switch the camera off," I called back to him. "You film me out here and it's going to get us both into a lot of trouble."

"Sure! Sure." He snapped the camera shut and caught up to me. "So, what's your name?"

"Mark."

"Pleasure to meet you." We shook hands, his feeling soft in my own, probably not used to hard work.

"Who do you work for?" I asked.

He took hold of my arm and halted our walk. "Look, I'll level with you. It's not the New York Times. You could say that I'm independent, but I've got contacts, good contacts back in the States."

I searched his face. Was he bullshitting me? Somehow I didn't think so. I'd missed talking with someone from my part of the world so I agreed. "On one condition." He nodded frantically, anything to get the story. "If you run the story, my name or image doesn't appear even after business here is concluded. It would be bad for both of us if it appeared. You understand?"

Kyle's face knotted in a frown, but he still agreed.

"And I'll need that in writing." It would be an empty guarantee, but couldn't hurt to have it.

"Of course."

"Have you eaten yet?" My stomach rumbled, pains of hunger reminding me how long it had been since food. I'd often had diarrhoea out here but not eating was a quicker way to get seriously ill.

"Not since this morning."

"We'll eat at the house. It's not far, come on."

We walked in silence. Kyle filmed our progress through Zorzor, the bullet ridden homes, the rusting hulks of vehicles, the numerous weapons held casually. He made sure to keep the camera off me.

Kyle gave an impressed whistle as we turned the corner and the manor came into sight. "You don't expect to see that here. It's like a nugget of gold in a pile of shit."

I laughed. It may have looked fancy compared to the rest of the town but the inside was run down and rotten. Most of the furniture had been looted when LURD rebels overtook Zorzor from government forces a month before. What was left was either too big to take, or decayed almost beyond use. Tiger King used the manor for his headquarters. He allowed me a small room on the second floor to sleep in. The choking reek of damp clung to the room constantly.

I placed a restraining hand on Kyle's chest. "If we see Tiger King only speak when spoken to. Show him respect at all times. You get me?"

Kyle nodded, still filming the manor house. He bounded up the three creaking steps, no hint of fear impeding him.

In the main room of the house, Tiger King sat with his feet outstretched, his AK-47 resting on his knees. He listened to some jazz music that played out in distorted tones on a small wireless radio. The heavy scent of pot hung in the air. A couple of his subordinates, dressed in loose vests, sat in the corner, also armed and smoking. They nodded to me but straightened at the sight of another white man. Tiger King's unfocused gaze settled on me, his movements lazy.

"Who is this man, Mak?"

"This is Kyle. He's a reporter."

Tiger King sat up. "Hey, reporter. Make me famous." He laughed and swept his AK to the ready. He pulled the slide back and let it go. Kyle flinched. First time in the field, I guessed.

"Take his bloody picture," I whispered to Kyle, who still hadn't moved. It didn't do to disappoint the rebel commander. If things went bad, my intervention would only go so far. I had seen this man in action, and I was a foreigner messing in Liberian business, a white man in a black man's war.

Kyle pulled a camera from his vest. The telescopic lens buzzed as he focused. His hands shook, making Tiger King smile.

Tiger King drew his machete, the polished blade gleamed through the smoke filled light. "You tell the world, Tiger King great warrior. He takes many skulls."

"Of … of course," Kyle said from behind the camera. He snapped a few more shots.

"Enough," I said. "We're hungry."

Tiger King stretched, the muscles on his arms flexing with the lethargic movement. Even such a slow movement seemed deadly.

I remembered how I'd first met Tiger King and the fear he instilled. He did everything to intimidate me, to ensure I knew he was King. I matched him with a front of hardly-felt bravery. Behind my sunglasses, the truth was clear in my eyes. I feared this man.

I owed the American nothing but didn't want to see him suffer. The commander shrugged, easing himself back into the wooden chair. He flexed his arm muscles, glistening with sweat. I pulled a packet of cigarettes from my tactical vest and threw them to him. He snatched them from the air, laughing. "Out back."

"Come on." I pulled Kyle, who still held his camera up.

"Is he always like that?" he asked when we were out of earshot.

"Yes. Look, you're new but you're not stupid. He is the worst kind of person you'll meet here. The muggers, murderers, rapists and all the other scum you're used to in the States … well, Tiger King is worse. He'll think nothing of hacking prisoners to death or beating his own men. Whatever he wants, smile and agree with him, however distasteful you find his actions. Smile and take his picture. He'd think nothing of killing you, or me for that matter. He is dangerous."

When I'd first met him, he was beating one of his own men with his rifle butt. I learned that he could be bought like most people in power in Liberia, or more so in his case, appeased. I've never smoked but I made sure to take plenty of cigarettes with me to trade. Sometimes what you could trade made the difference. Money was almost worthless. There wasn't anything to buy. The people had nothing.

We reached the back of the manor and stepped outside. A villager worked over an open fire, prodding the glowing embers with a stick. She didn't look at us once but handed out two steaming bowls of food from the pot above the fire, never meeting our eyes. Rice and stewed cassava leaf, spiced with some chilli. It was all Zorzor had to offer. Kyle sniffed at the meagre meal as I guided him back around the house. I liked to eat out on the porch where I could see some of the people of Zorzor go about their day.

"What is this shit?" asked Kyle.

"What you'll be eating for however long you stay in Liberia. It's all they have."

"Nice."

Sometimes a local would venture into the jungle and return with some fruit, but the immediate area had been stripped. Now they had to push deeper into the jungle, further from the safety of the town. I often wondered who these people were better off under. LURD or Taylor's government? LURD wouldn't execute them at random, but the rebels lived off these impoverished people with only the thin veneer of providing safety in return. The people had little and gave everything.

The wooden porch groaned under my weight as I sat. I pulled my AK off the sling and laid it next to me. I dug my fingers into the cassava stew and ate. The taste was so familiar that the flavour faded to almost nothing. Kyle rummaged through his bag and pulled out a pack of wet wipes. I couldn't help but laugh as he cleaned his hands. It was definitely his first time in the field. I looked at my own hands, covered in rice, dirt, and gun oil. Hygiene wasn't the priority here.

"What's so funny?" asked Kyle. He used a plastic picnic spoon to eat. "Holy shit, this tastes like ... shit." To his credit, he shovelled a second spoonful into his mouth.

"First time in the field?"

"No. Well, kinda, buddy," he said between mouthfuls. "I was in Kosovo but never left the UN compounds. This is my big break, or it better be. So you're a ... what? Merc?" he asked casually.

"No," I said, between clenched teeth. "I'm not."

"I'm sorry. It's just the rifle there, and you being the only white man here. I assumed you weren't here fighting for the great democratic cause."

"Mercenaries get paid to fight. I'm not here to fight."

"And the AK-47?"

"In case you hadn't noticed, there's a civil war going on. Only an idiot, or a reporter, walks into a warzone unarmed." I set down the empty bowl and pulled a bottle of water from my pocket, warmed by the jungle heat. "I'm here to train LURD rebels."

"So you're with the UK government?"

"You could say I'm independent. But I have contacts, good contacts all around."

Kyle laughed at the jibe and set aside his near-empty bowl. "You're a funny guy, buddy."

I passed him the bottle of water. He didn't complain about the temperature. He was learning.

I stretched out on the porch, fighting off the cramping in my legs. Six scrawny kids, dressed in clothes far too big, kicked a half-inflated football between them. Their enthusiastic laughter was a welcome change from the harsh cries and gunfire that haunted Zorzor. In another couple of years they'd, no doubt, be recruited into LURD ranks.

Kyle wiped his mouth with the back of his hand. "So, you want to get a little interviewing done?" he asked. "We can wait until later if it's better for you. No pressure."

Later, I'd have to inspect the new weapons and recruits, drill them and put them through their paces. But now I had a few hours to kill.

"Sure. I'll need the agreement, though." As much as I wanted to believe in a gentleman's accord, I'd learned a long time ago they were redundant in these times, especially with reporters. Nothing was stopping Kyle from leaving Liberia and spreading my name and picture about in the press. The more I thought about it, the more I knew that even with my insistence there was nothing stopping him. I wanted to trust Kyle. Time would tell.

"Great, bud. I gotta call the office before we start, just to make sure everything is cool at their end."

"Here." I threw him my satellite phone. "It's the best you'll get."

Kyle moved off the porch and around the corner, probably to speak in private. Without the AK strapped to my chest I felt naked. I reached out for it. I made the habit of having it within arm's reach at all times. Speaking with Kyle almost made me forget the constant presence of danger.

One of the children kicked the football too hard and it landed by my feet. They waved, smiling, wanting the ball back. I stood, teasing them twice with false kicks, before I sent it back. It struck me how long it'd been since I last kicked a football around.

Kyle returned with a broad smile. The children ran off with the ball. "It's done." He handed the phone back to me. "Your name and image won't appear in print. Just think of yourself as narrating what I film."

I tried to determine from his face whether he meant it. In the end, I didn't really care. I just wanted to talk.

"I'll film around here, the buildings, the kids and all that while you speak. You cool with that?" He took a seat beside me. "I could write it out but having it on tape, well, you know, makes sense."

"Sure." I drained the last of the hah-inducing water. Kyle set up the camera with an expert hand. I eased back into the shade of the porch. Kyle gave me the thumbs up, just off camera. He held a small wired microphone toward me. I pulled my sunglasses down over my eyes.

"So, you're not a mercenary. What are you doing in Liberia?"

Showtime. "I'm here to help train the LURD rebels and advise them on strategy when I can."

"You won't be taking part in any of the fighting?"

"Like I said, I'm not a mercenary. I'm not fighting for a cause, this weapon is only for personal defence. This is a civil war. A Liberian war, to be fought by Africans. The moment non-Africans become involved in the fighting it has far-reaching effects."

"You were hired by the LURD leadership? Was it just you?"

I slapped at a bug buzzing by my neck. "Our employers wish to remain anonymous, as you'd expect. There are eight of us. Seven stayed behind at the main rebel base and I volunteered to come forward so we could spread our experience over a wider area."

The bark of gunfire echoed from nearby. Kyle shot from his seat, eyes wild and searching for the source. "Just target practice or a celebration," I assured him. "There's no real fighting near Zorzor." He smiled, wiping the sweat from his face, and returned to his spot next to me.

"Hot damn, will they keep this shooting up all day?"

"And through the night," I told him. I now managed to block out the gunfire. One of the first things I'd suggested to Tiger King was the importance of reliable night sentries and the conservation of ammo. It went in one ear and out the other. I knew not to push the issue. Tiger King would fight the war the only way he knew how. We were miles behind the front lines but I had no confidence in the rebels' ability to hold a static front.

"Jesus. Right." Kyle took a sip of water, swirled it around his mouth, and then spat it into the dirt. "How would you respond to people who suggest you were profiting off the pain and suffering of others, a war profiteer if you will?"

I shrugged, having nothing to lose in answering. "Look, wars come and go. If anything, me being here will help shorten the war. Once the LURD are capable of ousting Taylor then the country can begin to heal and turn to democracy. No government death squads. No mass executions. No more war. The faster this happens the better. I didn't create the war, but indirectly, I'll help end it."

Kyle nodded, smoothing back the strands of his fringe, sticking to his sweat covered forehead. "I see. And what can you say about the child soldiers we've seen around the camp?"

If the last question cut close to the bone, this one was to the marrow. What surprised me was the anger that seemed directed at me within the question. Why was he angry with me? It felt like he blamed me for it. I answered truthfully. I wasn't the cause of the war. "It's a shame. Something which is distasteful, but look at it from an African perspective. It's easy to look in on events from the comfort of your armchair in the UK, in the States. This is how things are in Africa. I can't change it. The US can't change it. Only when things change for the better will child soldiers disappear. But it's a problem, I think, that will never fully disappear. No matter how much I wish it would. There will always be some stinking backwater in the world where children are forced to soldier."

"And you train them?" he all but spat out, his disgust blatant.

"Yes. I give them a chance to survive, for a while longer anyway. I do what I can."

Kyle and I stared at each other.

"Maybe we should take a break," he suggested.

"That would be good."

Kyle switched off the camera. I stood and stretched my back. My legs were cramping again, the pain like countless tiny hot needles pricking my skin. My health was suffering in Liberia. I no longer enjoyed the endurance I once had, the heat made it difficult to function. When possible, I tried to run once a day to keep in shape, but some days, motivation was difficult. If I held my hands out in front of me they would tremble, the diet didn't help matters.

"Look, buddy," said Kyle, halting me before I could take a walk. "I didn't mean to get angry with you there. That was a shitty thing to do. I'm sorry. It's just difficult, man, you know? To see kids with guns, knowing they'll see battle."

The anger was gone from his face and he was smiling. I pulled off my sunglasses. "It's ok. If there was any way I could stop them from using kids, I would. It's just a fact of African warfare. It happens. When I train them, I take them to the side, away from the men. I drill it into their heads to stay down. Stay in cover. I think I'm doing the right thing. I … hope I'm doing the right thing."

Kyle removed his photographer's vest and laid it by the camera. He pulled at the collar of his sweat-stained shirt. "What brought you out here in the first place? You don't seem like a war junkie. Ex-military?"

"Come on, I've got to take a walk. I need to stretch my legs a while."

"Good idea." Kyle carried his water with him, sipping as he listened to me speak.

"I've had military training, yes."

Kyle laughed. "You going to give me more than that?"

"Military counselling. That's what we do. And no, I'm not going to give you any more."

Kyle nodded, respecting my need for certain privacies. There were some things I wasn't ready to share. "I knew you weren't a war junkie. I could just tell." Kyle stopped and gazed out into Zorzor, his attention coming to rest at two cold men, painfully thin, sitting in the shadow of a dilapidated house. Everything about the town reeked of poverty, exacerbated by war. "They really are desperate, aren't they?"

"Yes, which is why the sooner the war is over, the better. Things will get better. It'll be slow but they will. What about you, then? What made you chase conflicts? And how did you get into Liberia? There's no direct way in"

"I told you, I have contacts. I came in through Guinea. As for photojournalism, well I majored in video media at college. I just wanted something different, y'know? I couldn't see myself working for a newspaper, writing about shit that doesn't matter. It's not like wars are going out of fashion anytime soon. Besides, war needs to be reported."

I was beginning to like Kyle. His honesty was refreshing as was his conversation. He represented a little piece of my former world, which I needed right then.

"You want to film me putting the new recruits through their paces?" I suggested.

"Sure, that'd be great," he said, with a smile. "Let me just go back to get my camera."

We went back to the manor and thankfully Kyle's equipment was untouched. The rebels were so used to looting that I feared the equipment may have been lifted by an opportunist. I should have considered this before we set out on our walk. The only reason they probably weren't was because they were left in the shadow of Tiger King's HQ. Thieves would be beaten or, if the mood fell across the commander, executed.

Kyle picked up his camera and pulled his vest back over his arms. As we walked to the edge of town where I drilled the recruits, he made a comment about my vest and how I must be uncomfortable in it.

"Better to be alive and miserable, than dead and comfortable." My vest held everything I needed. Ammo, med kit, satellite phone, antibiotics, and a GPS system.

The new recruits milled about in the clearing, watched over by some of the older rebels. I called over one of Tiger King's lieutenants, a grizzled toothless man, with streaks of grey in his hair and beard, and told him to gather the men and boys. Kyle stood next to me and whispered in my ear.

"Why do they have such wacky names?"

I shrugged. "It's just something they do. They like the theatrical, I suppose. Tiger King's brigade is called The Bloody Hand Boys. You'll hear a lot of names like that here."

"Will they mind me filming them?" Kyle asked.

"Just tell them you'll make them famous warriors."

Once the group of young warriors had assembled, no more than thirty to forty of them, I ran through my usual routine of giving a little speech. Two of the seasoned rebels handed out AKs to everyone else. I ignored the blank expressions on some of their faces. In many instances, I guessed it was the first time they'd ever held a weapon. The LURD projected the image of a volunteer organization, freedom fighters battling for the soul of the nation. In truth, some had been forced here. Just as they had been under President Taylor. Another sad fact of African warfare.

I showed them how to strip down the weapon, though none of them seemed to grasp it. Some of the weapons were filthy, but thankfully the AK-47 is a weapon that needs little maintenance and is reliable even in the worst hands.

Next, I showed them the RPG rocket launcher. Some of the recruits cheered when they saw the weapon. The RPG was pivotal in Liberian battles. Neither LURD nor the government forces would fight without it. I gave basic instruction in its use. Then, turning, I fired one rocket, like I'd done dozens of times, into the specially cleared area to the east of town. The grenade exploded against some rocks, throwing up debris, a hundred metres away. Again the men cheered, and I forced a smile to give them confidence in a weapon I held little confidence in. It was inaccurate and as deadly to friendly forces as it was to the enemy. I handed the smoking launcher to an excited young man. Toothless and malnourished, he rushed to take possession of the weapon.

I turned to Kyle and pointed to his camera. "This man is going to make you famous. You're in The Bloody Hand Boys now!" The recruits cheered, waving their weapons and dancing. One man fired off several rounds in the air. I instinctively ducked at the sudden outburst.

I walked over to Kyle, who searched for the source of the fire, his eyes darting about. I pointed over to the group of rebels. He shook his head, mouthed a curse.

"Thanks. That was a nice touch," he said. "Is that all the training they will get?"

"Depends on what Tiger King decides. If he holds them here for a few more days, then that's better for everyone. If they're needed out in the fighting then that's it. I do what I can."

Kyle swore. He filmed the recruits firing off at the boulder in the clearing. Their aim was terrible, but with precious little ammunition for them to practice with, I didn't hold much hope for improvement. A few times I questioned what good my being there did, but LURD leadership were happy, the money flowed to the company, so I stayed and did the job I was paid to do.

"Shit, buddy. They're terrible shots."

"I know." I waved over to the lieutenant, cutting my hand across my throat. It was enough ammo wasted for today. The shooting came to an end and Kyle released a breath. He panned the camera onto me, filming my legs, and feet, protecting my identity.

"So, what weapons do you have?"

I wasn't prepared, but I tried to seem natural. Pulling the AK from my back, I showed it to the camera. "AK-47 with collapsible stock. Not what I would choose.

I'm used to using MP5s, you know, more personal defence weapons than assault rifles, but I needed something that used the same type of ammunition as everyone else." I patted my leg. "Glock 17. Something I've taken with me. Added protection."

"Sweet."

"Come on, we'll go back to the HQ."

Kyle put his camera away. He snapped a few stills of the recruits before he joined me. We were talking about New York and Kyle's flat when I heard a sound I couldn't place. A sound so foreign to Zorzor it made me halt.

"Mark? What's wrong?"

"Mortars!" I heard three in quick succession, *thoomb thoomb thoomb.*

"So what? They're wasting ammo again?"

"No! We don't have mortars. Fuck me. Get down."

I grabbed Kyle by his vest, throwing him into the shadow of a house. I dived in after him. A heartbeat later, the mortar rounds struck. The explosions were deafening and close, much louder than the RPG explosion minutes before.

"What the shit's going on?" Kyle was wide-eyed, like a panicked animal. "Are we under attack?"

I ignored him and cried out to the rebels, "Contact!" I edged my way to the corner of the house. Kyle tried to follow but I pushed him back against the wall. Slowly, I inched my head around the corner. People were screaming, women were running in every direction. Chaos reigned. No one was sure what was going on. I had a line of sight to where I'd left the recruits. One or more of the mortar rounds had struck the group. Torn and shredded bodies lay about a blackened area of the road. One woman, covered in dirty and debris gave a hoarse scream, her hands clutching at her guts, failing to keep them inside her torn body. My heart was racing, and I struggled with the urge to run. All the training in the world can never prepare you for this.

Run, or stay and fight? In my mind, I ran through the training I received like a prayer. I stayed.

"Back!" I screamed to the exposed rebels. "Get back to cover!" I pulled my AK to my hands, flipping out the stock, and thumbed the safety off. Some of the recruits ran back toward the buildings and walls but a PK machine gun opened up from the jungle. "How the fuck did government troops get here?" I muttered to myself.

"I need to film this shit."

"Stay back!"

Most of my new recruits lay dead or dying. The PK gunner had taken care of those that ran. Two more mortar rounds hit the teaching area. The blast concussion scorched me like heat from a furnace. A brief and searing heat pulverising the bodies into a mismatch of innards and bone fragments. A third mortar struck a house fifty metres behind us. It splintered the iron roof and blew holes out of the wall. Shards of shrapnel hit all around us. They lost most of the inertia to cause any real damage. I chanced a look at Kyle. He was pale and sweating, but filming where the mortar hit. It was close, too close. I looked at the jungle again and saw figures moving in the foliage. The machine gunner must have stopped to reload.

"Kyle, you should head back to HQ. Go now. I'll keep you safe."

"No fuckin' way, man. This is what I came here for."

I didn't have time to argue. If he wanted to stay then that was his choice. I looked back into town. The LURD rebels were moving toward us, Tiger King driving them on like cattle. Some small-arms fire erupted from the jungle, followed by a salvo of RPGs. I couldn't see where they landed, but heard them pop nearby. The PK started up again. We needed a heavy machine gun. The rebels could have racked the tree line to gain fire superiority.

"Get to cover and fire back!" I cried out to the surviving rebels.

Tiger King ignored my repeated cries, drove his fighters into the storm of bullets instead, and left behind those who fell. The rebels fired a few RPGs toward the jungle. At least the mortars had stopped.

Kyle was on his stomach, his camera held out just beside my knee. Two LURD warriors rushed forward but were gunned down, their bodies torn apart by the high calibre rounds. Two rounds snapped off the wall above our heads. I ducked and Kyle squealed, dropping his camera. It landed a few feet from our cover, out in the open.

"Why aren't you shooting back?"

I wasn't a mercenary. I wasn't here to fight. But I was in danger and no matter how I felt about it. It was them or me.

"My camera. Grab my camera," he pleaded.

I chanced a look around the corner. I could see one government fighter spraying around us with automatic fire. The rounds kicked up dirt and splintered the wall. I put the rifle to my shoulder and shot at the fighter. My rounds took him in the leg and he fell, clutching his wound. I stepped from cover, and grabbed the camera handle, and pulled it back with me. I'm not sure if the man lived or died, but my stomach churned in a painful crush at the prospect.

"Take your camera."

"Thanks, buddy," Kyle said, patting my shoulder. I squeezed off a few more shots at where the PK fire was coming from. It didn't stop the onslaught.

Tiger King's voice somehow rang over the battle. "Go! Go! Show them how my warriors fight." He stood behind a line of LURD racing toward the battle, between two houses. Naked from the waist up except for the ammo belts crossing his body, he held his AK in one hand and an RPG in the other. His dark, muscled torso glistened with sweat.

LURD fighters were filtering through the buildings, moving up to fight. At least they had learned to stay in cover. A few more of our RPGs flew into the undergrowth. To my left, I saw a LURD soldier. He couldn't have been more than ten, standing with his rifle, out of cover. The weapon didn't even have a magazine in it. Tears streaked his face. I called to him, urged him, begged him to come to me. Our eyes met and for a second he took a step my way. I don't know if it was terror or the words of Tiger King, but he remained still.

The PK gunner trained his weapon him on him and raked his tiny form with bullets. The rounds tore his legs apart and he fell. I watched. There was nothing I could do. A smaller bullet, probably from an AK, struck him in the head. Part of his skull exploded out the back of his head in a bloody cloud. The worst part was hearing him moan after it happened. The moaning went on for some time. I think Kyle got the boy's death on camera, but I didn't ask and he didn't volunteer the information.

I fired a whole magazine into the trees, more out of anger than anything else. I reloaded the weapon as more of our RPGs began to strike the enemy position. A figure leaped over the wall behind our position, landing hard next to us. Jacob, a teenage fighter was high or drunk, probably both. Twice I had to push him back from rushing the jungle and meeting certain death. He stood and fired relentlessly into the trees. "I'm great warrior," he kept repeating.

At last the PK fell silent. It turned out that the government troops had enough and were retreating.

"Now! Go! Go!" boomed Tiger King. The rebels burst from hiding, rushing the trees.

"Don't let them go too far. Ambushes!" I called.

Tiger King ignored me, running after his fighters. I gave up trying to stop Jacob from going. He ran off, firing into the air as he went. Kyle started to stand, but I pulled him down.

"Could be a trap. Stay here and film if you have to, but keep your fucking head down! There could be snipers."

He nodded, but said nothing. I caught him glancing at the child's body. I would have covered him up, but I had nothing to do it with. He would be one of many bodies very soon. The contact lasted around twenty minutes before the gunfire died down. The LURD had probably pushed the government forces back. "Okay, let's go back to HQ. You all right?"

Kyle nodded. We ran back to HQ. I kept my weapon at the ready and my free hand on Kyle's back, pushing him along. We reached HQ without incident. The manor house survived the battle unscathed. We sat in our earlier positions on the porch. Neither of us spoke. Kyle looked down at the dirt and I cleaned my AK.

"How do you do it?" His voice had lost all emotion.

"Do what?"

"This?" He waved a hand around at the carnage. "See children gunned down. See people die. I've filmed bodies before but this … this is something different."

I shrugged, the motion seeming uncaring and harsher than I meant it. "This is Liberia. That's how it is." I didn't know the words to say to make it better. I couldn't even tell him how I dealt with it, I just did. I let the numbness take care of it.

He chewed the inside of his mouth. "That kid, he couldn't have been more than twelve. Killed like that."

"I know. If I could have saved him, I would have."

"It just seems so pointless. All of it. Just a waste."

"That's what war is," I said. I wasn't angry with Kyle, but I transferred the anger of the boy's death onto him for lack of a better target. "We fight now so others will never have to." I didn't believe it. I'd heard it somewhere and it seemed appropriate to fill the void that no words could really fill. I remembered something Plato once said, 'Only the dead have seen the end of war'.

We sat in silence. My stomach ached and I had to go to the trench to shit out my bowels. When I returned, Kyle was looking in the direction of the centre of Zorzor. There was a commotion over on the right side of town. "What's that, Mark?"

"I'm not sure, but it won't be anything good. Listen, I don't think you should go and see whatever it is."

Kyle had his camera out, turning to the source of the noise. "Why? It's what I came to see."

"They've probably captured someone. It gets a little harsh." I'd seen it once and it made me fear Tiger King more than I did already.

"I'd better go and see. It's my job." He was looking to me for the nod of approval, as if his actions required my blessing.

I shook my head. The last thing I wanted to see was Tiger King's bloody handiwork again. "Shit, you really don't know what's happening over there." I sighed. "Look, I'll go with you, but both of us will regret it." I don't know why I agreed to go. I wanted to protect Kyle. The shock and horror in his eyes had once been me. Perhaps I wanted him to retain something that I was missing.

We walked to the gathering, a clearing of dusty emptiness. A car husk lay rusting beside the men. The prisoner was stripped naked, the jeering crowd holding him by his arms. Machetes, bayonets and rifle barrels were thrust into him. He bled from several wounds on his body. A long, jagged cut on his arm bled profusely. From where I stood, his eyes seemed to be all whites. Kyle looked on, camera in hand. Tiger King marched up to him, his polished machete resting over his shoulder. He spoke to the prisoner, whatever he said lost in the noise of the crowd. The prisoner thrashed around and Tiger King reached down, taking hold of his manhood. With two short, sharp slashes, he cut it free then stuffed it into the prisoner's mouth. The crowd went wild and they fell on the man. He disappeared under the press of bodies. Bayonets and machetes ended his life in a visceral slaughter.

I turned to Kyle and pulled him away from the scene. He switched the camera off and put it away in its protective case as we headed back to HQ.

"You did nothing," Kyle said, without emotion, his voice reduced to a single dull tone.

"That's right. I told you once before, it's Tiger King's way. If I had tried to stop it, it would have been you or me, even both of us that Tiger King was butchering. When I say 'this is Liberia,' this is what I mean. You can't change it. Sometimes you can't even accept it. What happened here should never happen, ever. But it does. Don't think you can walk in here with good intentions and change how things are. Maybe in ten, twenty, or fifty years, this will never happen again. Maybe. And now you have a story to tell. War, to most people, is something they see on TV. Tell this story better. Let the world see that it needs to stop this."

Kyle seemed like he was about to cry. He sucked down great gulps of cordite and blood-tainted air. "You saved my life back there."

"I didn't do anything."

"You did. Listen. Before, I would have released the video, your name and all, just for this story. I'm sorry, but I would've. I needed this, really did. But now, hell, your name and image is safe."

"I appreciate your honesty. The company don't like unwelcome attention, let's just say that."

"I understand, buddy." He used the nickname without irony for the first time. "So, what will you do now?"

"If Tiger King has any sense he'll move forward, clear the jungle of any more government surprises. If he does, I'll go with him. If not, I'll stay here and train the rebels some more. Maybe now Tiger King will accept the need for patrols." I shrugged. "Who knows?"

Night was drawing in fast. We stood in the weak light cast from the manor house, a swarm of insects above our heads. "I'd like to stay in contact with you, Mark," said Kyle.

"I'd like that." I gave him the satellite phone number, adding, "If I don't pick up, I'm either dead or under fire."

He gave a polite laugh. I didn't say anything, not sure if he understood my dark humour.

"Well, it's been one shitty night. I think I'll hit the sack."

"Sleep in my room. I've got a mattress, a shit one, but it's better than the floor. There's an insect net, too. I've got to speak to Tiger King."

"Thanks, buddy." He shook my hand, then in a sudden move, pulled me in and embraced me. We slapped each other on the back. Kyle began the climb up the steps to the manor house when I called out to him, "Hey, I've a title for your film, or article, or whatever the hell you're making."

"Hit me," said Kyle, weariness heavy in his eyes.

"Only The Dead Have Seen The End Of War. A Liberian Story."

"I like it. A little long, though. How about, 'Only The Dead?'"

"It fits."

"Goodnight, Mark. And thanks."

"Goodnight."

The next day, Tiger King received orders to pull his forces back. It seemed the rebels had lost control of the strategic town of Tubmanburg. Could things get any worse?

Chapter Two

I spent most of the night in conversation with Tiger King and his lieutenants. It wasn't easy to forget what happened to the prisoner, but as the evening went on, it became just another reason to fear Tiger King.

The room, thick with the heavy scent of pot made it difficult to keep a clear mind. We talked about tactical issues and the next steps to take against the government. It was either the effects of the pot or the comedown from the battle, I fell asleep in the chair. My dreams were terrible. Worse than any imagined nightmare my mind was capable of creating. This dream's horror came from worldly experience. I saw the child gunned down, his eyes fixed on me as he mouthed something I couldn't hear. I woke with the child's face scorched into my mind.

Tiger King's satellite phone was ringing. The happy little jingle out of place in a room full of armed killers. I wiped the sweat from my forehead. I stood and stretched. My neck seized up and my knees were stiff. They popped with my movement. I decided to leave Tiger King to his call. I got as far as the doorway when Tiger King's voice boomed in curses.

"Mak! Come here."

"What?" I turned but stayed near the door. I needed a piss and wasn't in the mood for any of his shit.

"We retreat."

"What?"

He waved me over to his table and the black and white map of Liberia, his only tactical aid in the room. He explained, with lazy movements, how we were to pull back from Zorzor to a more defendable position. Tubmanburg, a strategically important town in the south, had fallen and government forces were filtering through the jungle right now. If we didn't pull out in the next few hours, Zorzor would be under siege. With little ammo, or promise of reinforcements, our position was untenable. Tiger King finished by stabbing the map with his knife. He left it shuddering in the table, the excess of his brutality carrying over into his planning.

"One hour, Mak."

Now it was my turn to swear. I ran from the room and straight out the back door. A woman carrying a bundle of linen screamed when I burst from the manor house. I held up a hand and offered a smile. She shook her head and carried on. It rained in a sticky haze, not quite a downpour but I knew the signs. It would rain today, and hard.

I didn't have time to visit the latrine trench so I just unzipped and pissed where I stood, not looking down. I was suffering with scabies and the effects on my dick wasn't something to dwell on. Once, I heard someone refer to it as 'The Seven Year Itch'. It was an appropriate name, it felt like I spent most of my downtime scratching the rash. It was an easy thing to contract out in Liberia, wading through dirty water was probably where I'd caught it, or from one of the many dirty bodies around town.

I finished pissing and headed back into the house, to my room, and found Kyle snoring beneath the insect net. Like a cartoon miser, he slept on the filthy mattress with his camera bag clutched to his chest. There was an odd smell in the room. It took me a moment to realise what it was. Next to his bag, outside the net was a Lynx deodorant can. The sweet scent seemed odd and out-of-place here. It cast my mind back to gym class at school. I laughed. Kyle must be the only man to bring deodorant into a warzone. I dreaded to think how bad the rest of Zorzor smelt to Kyle.

"Hey, sleeping beauty. Time to get up."

Kyle opened his eyes. "Aw come on, buddy. No offense, but your face isn't what I wanted to wake up to."

"Yeah, well we've got trouble."

Kyle sat up, laying his camera bag to the side. He cracked his neck and yawned. "What kind of trouble."

"The worst kind. We have to pull out of Zorzor. Seems like LURD went and lost control of Tubmanburg. We've got government forces heading this way. If we don't go now, we'll be trapped."

"That's bad then?"

"Only if you don't mind dying in the next day or so."

"Actually, I do." Kyle pulled himself from under the net. In his underwear he stretched out and then touched his toes. "So what's the plan?" He pulled on his clothes.

"I'm going to get you to one of the jeeps and send you out now. You'll get through before the government forces close the road.

"I like it. What about you, though?"

I shrugged. "I stay with Tiger King and the men. We can't follow the road. Too slow. We'll filter through the jungle and make it back to the border that way."

Kyle, now fully dressed, hurried to pack all his things into his bag. His equipment and personal effects were more than one man could carry. I went to the window and pulled my bag from under the rotted desk. Everything was packed. I lived out of my backpack, ready to bug-out at a moment's notice. I wished Kyle had been the same. It took him awhile to get his shit together. I stood urging him to hurry, helping throw things into his bags when I could. I'm not sure if Kyle grasped the seriousness of the impending siege. It was forefront in my mind.

He zipped up his last bag. "Ready to go."

There were two backpacks and three holdalls. I picked up my own pack and slung it over my shoulder. I rested the AK on my front; the weight on the sling felt especially heavy today. I picked up as much as I could and Kyle took the rest. We left the small room behind, my home for several weeks. I wasn't sad to leave the manor house. It held too many bad memories. There had been too many nights spent listening to the screams of the wounded and the raped. Tiger King was cruel to his men, and worse to the people of Zorzor when it suited him.

We stepped out onto the front porch. The news of the retreat spread in the time I'd been with Kyle. Soldiers and villagers were running, frantic to complete whatever task they'd been assigned. Some carried bundles, others struggled with valuables. If there was any order to it, I couldn't see it.

"What will happen to the villagers, Mark? Will they come with us?"

"I don't know." I didn't want to talk. Kyle slowed as he spoke and watched the villagers. I kept urging him on, it was an annoying habit he developed. When Kyle talked, progress slowed. We came to the road which stretched off into jungle, back toward Guinea. Two of the pickups were gone. The third was a wreck, doors open and the hood popped up. I dropped the bags, ignoring Kyle's protests about fragile equipment. The vehicle had been stripped down. I circled it; parts of the engine were missing. One of the tires was punctured and deflated.

"Motherfuckers!" I said, slamming the hood down.

"Damn. That's bad," said Kyle, setting down his burden. "What now?"

Tiger King came marching up, many of his soldiers following. Among them, some villagers were acting as baggage handlers, probably not by choice. Kyle began snapping a few pictures of the army beginning to retreat. The rain became more adamant, and Kyle held a hand over the lens shielding it. The question he asked earlier stuck in my mind. What would happen to the villagers? When the government took Zorzor, they'd surely exact a heavy toll for the village supporting LURD rebels. As much as I wanted to help the people who endured the LURD occupation, there was nothing I could do.

"What now?" Kyle kept snapping as the soldiers moved past us. Tiger King strode toward us, his body glistening in the rain. He smiled despite the impending retreat. Kyle brought the camera away from his eye as Tiger King looked at him. Kyle dropped his gaze to the ground.

"We go now, Mak!" Tiger King commanded. He pointed with his machete toward the jungle. "You come with us."

"Fine. I need someone to help us with these bags."

Tiger King boomed out a laugh, shaking his head. He put a cigarette to his lips. "No one help you." He shielded the lighter from the rain, and lit his smoke.

In my mind, I threw every curse I could think of at him.

Tiger King waved his troops into the jungle, shoving those who were moving too slow. Many carried ammunition or beaten plastic containers of clean water. Most passing me were young, their burdens too heavy to make the speed their commander desired. Tiger King punched a boy of around twelve in the head. He collapsed, dropping the water container, which burst. I turned away as he started to kick his young soldier. Kyle didn't dare snap a picture. The boy screamed.

"You've got three minutes to make a decision on what comes with us and what stays," I shouted.

Kyle blinked like he didn't understand the words. "I need everything, buddy."

"Take two bags and the third we'll fill with water and a little rice."

"I can't do that."

"Look," I said, struggling with my temper. "We've got a long trek through the jungle, you're not in the best shape and I sure as hell won't be able to carry all that shit. Take what you need, nothing else."

"Christ, I didn't think it would come to this."

Kyle dropped to his knees and started rifling through his bags. He tossed aside equipment and the odd smaller camera. I turned back and scanned the direction where the government forces attacked from the day before. That's where they would come from again. I watched for the slightest movement, the slightest sign of immediate danger. So far nothing. Tiger King had grown tired of the beating and disappeared into the jungle.

"Hurry up. One minute."

Kyle waved without looking up.

I walked over to the beaten boy. He was a pitiful sight, looking like a victim of a hit and run. His jaw was broken and hung redundant to the left. His nose a pulped mess, the blood from it covering his mouth and chin. Tiger King kicked him so hard he'd left the imprint of his boot treads on his body. A tiny hand reached up to me. He made weak clicking sounds, his tongue moving but not able to form words. I took his hand, there was little strength there, like a brittle branch from a tree. His eyes never left mine, they were dull and full of pleading.

"Be brave," I whispered. He blinked once. I put my hands under him and as gently as I could, lifted him into my arms. He mewed at the movement. Tears streaked down his face, smearing the blood there. I sprinted back to where Kyle still rummaged through his possessions. The boy bounced around in my grasp, his arms unable to hold onto me for support.

"I'm just done." Kyle turned toward me, noticing the burden in my arms. "What's going on? Is that the boy who Tiger King beat on?

I nodded.

"He looks pretty bad. What are you going to do with him?"

"Wait here. I need to get him back into town."

"Are you crazy? I thought you said we needed to leave as-soon-as."

"I'll be a couple of minutes at best."

Kyle glanced back into town. "This is crazy, buddy. What if the government guys show up just now?"

"What should I do?" I turned to show Kyle the limp boy. "You want me to leave him out here, out in the open?"

"It's not that … it's just …"

"There." I motioned with the boy to where Tiger King and the rest had disappeared into the jungle. "If you don't want to wait, that's fine. That's where you go. Just follow the trail and you'll catch up to the rest of them." I didn't wait for the reply. Kyle said something but I didn't hear it. I was already jogging back into Zorzor. With my pack and the boy to carry, I was slower than usual. Progress seemed to drag out and the boy kept slipping. I scanned the jungle on the far side of town as I paused to wipe some sweat out of my eyes. Some villagers still milled about town, wide-eyed. They looked at me with curiosity. I didn't have the luxury of time to stop, so I carried on, back toward the manor house. A few faces peered out of doorways at me, mostly old men, and women with children. Each were hampered by circumstance to stay in Zorzor. Those who were fit enough would probably seek some shelter in the jungle around town. They'd probably last the night before the government forces found them.

The manor was quiet, it was only when I walked into the house that the soft cries of the wounded could be heard. I went to the main room where Tiger King and I had discussed strategy, while he polluted the air with pot. There were three people lying on the floor, one covered by a blood stained sheet; blackened feet poked out the bottom. I called out for someone to come and help the boy. Nobody answered. I went through the other rooms, only the low moans of the wounded waited for me. It seems that once Tiger King left, the people of Zorzor decided to move their wounded to more comfortable quarters. Nobody tended to them. It wasn't really a surprise.

I couldn't take the child with me; he'd die in the jungle, his wounds quickly succumbing to infection. There was no option other than to leave him here. I climbed the stairs to my old bedroom and found my mattress and insect net untouched. I'd neglected to pack it up when we left. I laid the boy onto the bed, he cried like a wounded animal with the motion. It was a grotesque sight. At least he could lay in some comfort at the manor instead of dying in agony trekking through the jungle.

The only other thing I could do for the boy was to strip him of anything which suggested he was a soldier. I took his ammo and the bandanna that some LURD wore to identify themselves as part of The Bloody Hand Boys. There was nothing else I could do for him. He had a dark bruise on his right shoulder from firing the AK. I hoped the government forces would mistake this bruise for one that Tiger King gave him.

"I'm sorry, kid. You didn't deserve this." I pulled my canteen and using a little water, started to wash down his face, dabbing the bandanna to clean the blood. I used light touches around the nose and jaw. I wish I could've done more. "I'm sorry."

I stood but before I could turn, the boy raised his hand toward me. It shook from the effort, the fingers slowly grasping for me. It was one of the most difficult things I've had to do in my life. I turned and walked from the room. The sounds of his soft moaning filtered through the hallway. It was too much. I ran, taking the stairs three at a time, and then burst from the front door. The rain was coming down heavier. I stood there letting myself get soaked. I forced my breathing to return to normal. Not for the first time, I asked myself why I was in Liberia at all.

A woman screamed. For a moment, I couldn't trace where the sound came from. Gunfire broke the calm of the rainstorm. I unhooked my AK, pulled out the stock, and flipped it off safety. This time I didn't have the benefit of

Tiger King and The Bloody Hand Boys as back-up. I may have held the only LURD weapon left in Zorzor. Sliding along the wall of the manor house, I popped my head out of cover. In the tree line, like the day before, there were men filtering through the jungle, and firing their weapons.

I didn't wait. Didn't consider strategy or cover. I ran, with fear giving me wings. No heavy machine guns yet, thankfully. More screaming but I left them all behind.

Kyle was standing by the wrecked pickup when I arrived back, two holdalls by his feet. There was photography equipment littering the ground. He waved me over.

"It's under attack?"

I didn't stop to speak, I just pushed him toward the trail into the jungle. He barely had time to retrieve his bags. We reached the trees and I had to stop, my hands on my knees. A fire burned in my chest, tears stinging my eyes.

"Well, do you feel better for that?" Kyle asked.

"Yes," I gasped.

"I think you did the right thing, buddy. I just got scared back there, that's all. Did the kid survive?"

"I think so." My breathing calmed down, almost to normal. "Right, you need to get going. We need to put some distance between us and them. Just keep on this trail, don't wander off and you'll catch up with the column."

"You're not coming?" Kyle's eyes were wide.

"I need to collect some intel on the government forces. I'll be ten minutes behind you, I promise."

He started to protest, but I pushed him away with more force than I really intended.

"Go!"

I watched him race off into the jungle and then flattened myself just off the trail, the undergrowth providing me with a little cover. The soil sunk under my weight. The sound of the rain battering against the foliage became so loud, it was almost deafening.

I observed Zorzor for fifteen minutes, watching government troops move into the town. Longer than I intended. I was about to leave when the sight of flames caught my eye. The manor house was fast being consumed by fire, a thick oily smoke rising into the air. The boy was dead. I knew how ruthless the government forces are, they burned all the wounded inside the house. My stomach sank. I pushed myself up from the soil. If I was lucky, they would spend some time sacking Zorzor before pursuing us. If not, we would be overtaken and executed before nightfall. I spat, and then took off after Kyle and the others. Farewell Zorzor. Rest in peace.

Chapter Three

It took twenty minutes to catch up with Kyle and the retreating LURD. For a big guy, he moved quickly when needed. With his back to me I stepped next to him and grabbed one of his bags.

"Jesus," he said between laboured breaths. "You scared the shit out of me."

"Sorry."

The retreating Bloody Hand Boys halted for a moment. Tiger King was at the head of the column, his powerful voice could be heard over the driving rain. Kyle sank down to the ground on his knees, ignoring the damp earth. He didn't even bother to take off his backpack. His cheeks were ruddy and his chest heaved. I sat his bag down next to him. Some of the rain managed to penetrate the jungle canopy, a steady drip landed on my shoulder. I moved under the trickle, letting the cool water fall over my face and mouth. Best to save the bottled water for when we would surely need it.

"You were away for longer than I thought," said Kyle. "It took me a while to catch up with the rest of them, probably because I was checking over my shoulder every five seconds." Kyle wiped the sweat from his brow with the back of his hand. "So what happened to Zorzor?"

"The manor house was on fire when I left. I don't think the government forces will be after us until tomorrow, they've got a town to sack."

"The kid you took back to town?"

I shook my head.

Kyle seemed to chew at the inside of his mouth for a moment, then nodded twice. "Sorry about that, buddy. I know you wanted to save him."

My voice rasped with dryness, "Yeah." I cleared it before continuing. "I doubt he would have survived." I tried to make it sound offhand, flippant almost.

"Tiger King's a real piece of shit."

I nodded. Part of me was too tired to speak. The other part didn't want to give any more thought to Tiger King and those who suffered under his yoke.

"What happens now?" Kyle craned his neck to look up the column. "It doesn't seem like we have a clear route ahead of us."

I followed his gaze. Up ahead, an animated Tiger King pointed into denser jungle with his machete. One of his lieutenants stood with him, nodding, his AK barely lowered, pointed at the watching troops. I knew where we needed to go, just not how we would get there. Kyle looked up at me, expecting answers. He travelled to Zorzor in relative comfort. Getting away would be an ordeal, probably worse than anything else he had suffered in his life. I pulled my GPS from my tac vest, then squatted down next to him. The screen was slightly cracked, but it still worked.

"You remember Voinjama? It would have been the first city you visited when you crossed from Guinea."

Kyle levered himself up on an elbow so he could see the screen. "I passed through Voinjama, briefly. Was a dump from what I saw. A lot of armed men."

I nodded. "That is where LURD operate from. If they're able to turn the momentum of the government forces, it'll be from there. Now, to get there we need to cross a few rivers. We'll come to the first in a few days, I should think. It's difficult to judge on foot."

"I take it there isn't a handily placed bridge or two on our way."

"In the middle of the jungle? There will be shallower areas where we can wade through. If not, we follow the course of the rivers until we find a road and hope that government forces aren't there ahead of us. It's a long way through rough terrain to Voinjama from here, and we can't afford to take it easy."

"How many days in the jungle?"

I looked at the ragged column at rest. I didn't want to add to Kyle's troubles so I gave him a generous estimation. "Five days at the most." We would likely be playing cat and mouse with our pursuers and battling another enemy as dangerous as the government troops: the jungle. Up until now, progress had been steady, but we'd hardly begun.

Kyle swore, wiping the moisture from his forehead again. He pulled the canteen from his pack and drank. We couldn't risk waiting for much longer. There was every chance that some elements of the government forces were already in pursuit. If they were racing forward on the roads, we were in danger of having our escape route strangled.

"Go easy on that water, you don't want to puke it up." I stood, my knees giving a loud pop at the movement. "Be ready to move soon. We can't linger here for long."

Kyle saluted with his canteen, touching it to his forehead.

"I need to speak with Tiger King," I said wiping the persistent rain from my face.

I trudged through the narrow clearing. All eyes followed me as I made my way. It was unusual to hear the LURD so quiet, usually they sang or greeted me with a wave and a shout. They just sat there watching me, like I had all the answers to questions they didn't want to ask. The weight of retreat rested heavily on all our shoulders.

"Ah, Mak!" roared Tiger King. "Let me see that computer."

I handed the GPS over to him. He studied it for a moment, like a professor thinking profound thoughts. We had to move. Suggesting ideas to Tiger King was a risky move, he was a loose cannon. He would either accept the idea, somehow convincing himself it was his own, or he would throw it back in my face.

"We're here." I pointed to our position on the screen. "And we need to get to here." I pushed my finger to Voinjama.

"I know this, Mak."

He handed back the GPS, then crossed his arms. I leaned in closer, so his lieutenant wouldn't overhear. "We need to move. The enemy will be close behind."

"Then we fight them here!" His voice was loud, many of the rebels turned to watch. "We fight them here!" he cried again, his arms outstretched, machete in one hand and a steel-plated Beretta in the other.

"Those weren't your orders," I hissed. I should have considered my words better.

Tiger King swung at me with the flat of the machete blade. The blade slapped my chest, making me step back a couple of feet. "Tiger King is commander!"

What happened in the next few moments was a gamble on my part. I rushed back in front of him, my words full of force which I didn't feel. "If you fight and die now, nobody will know of your bravery. They'll think you were slaughtered with the women in Zorzor."

He stepped closer, his machete raised, poised to swing again, this time, the edge toward me.

"Get to Voinjama! Kill the enemy there in front of an audience! Let everyone know how brave you are!"

He stood there, his dark eyes never leaving my own. He ran his tongue over his lips and then slowly dropped his arm. I kept my eyes on his. To do otherwise would be a show of weakness. And probably fatal.

"Yes. We go to Voinjama. Now!" He looked me up and down once and then turned, marching over to his lieutenant.

His order caused a silent reaction with the rebels. They went about picking up their burdens, getting ready to march. My hand was still on my Glock, as it had been throughout the confrontation. If he so much as looked like he was about to swing the machete, I was prepared to shoot. It would have resulted in a violent and prolonged death for Kyle and me later at the hands of his lieutenants, but I wouldn't have let him cut me down.

I headed back to the rear of the column, where Kyle stood watching. Shaking, I balled my fists trying to control the trembles. The smeared mud splattering Kyle's face contrasted sharply with his skin.

"Jesus, I thought you were …"

I held up a hand to silence him, I couldn't talk yet. He waited patiently, blinking until I was able to speak again. "I'm fine," I somehow managed to say. "Get your shit together and get going."

The rebels were already starting to penetrate into the thicker jungle, leaving the relatively well-travelled path.

"What about you?"

"I just need a minute. I'll be right behind you."

Kyle didn't say anything else, he picked up his bags and struggled after the ragtag army, retreating into the swallowing jungle. I sat down on a fallen tree trunk. Rotten, it sank inwards under my weight. There, alone and with the Liberian jungle creaking around me, I cried. Bitter angry tears. They flooded out of me and I didn't try and stop them.

I cried my last tear, looking behind, back into the jungle. I knew they weren't far behind. Wiping my face down and smoothing back my hair, I set off after Kyle and the rebels.

Chapter Four

After my moment of emotion in the clearing, I felt better. I left the guilt behind, lost in jungle, lost in a place I would try to never return to. My mind was now focused on staying alive. The column made little progress since leaving the track. The jungle proved difficult in places to pass. From ahead, the sound of ringing blades filtered back to me. Again, I found Kyle at the rear, struggling with his bags.

"Good to see you, buddy," he said, a smile breaking through the mask of mud he wore. "You okay?"

I nodded. "What's going on up ahead? Why have they stopped?"

Kyle shrugged. "Think they're having to hack through something." He handed me one of his bags with a sheepish smile. I accepted it without comment. "What happens now?"

"We move as fast as we can away from Zorzor, across those rivers I mentioned, then onto Voinjama."

"You make it sound so easy."

"It'll be fine as long as we keep moving. We can't afford these delays."

Kyle and I lapsed into silence. While we waited, he searched through his bag, occasionally pulling out a piece of photography equipment and inspecting it. I kept searching back the way we came, always scanning for our first sign of pursuit. The thing about the jungle is that it's never still. It's impossible to feel completely alone. Often I found myself seeing flashes of movement. Large insects buzzed about my face. Not ten feet away the serpentine body of a snake slipped through the low hanging branches. The jungle had a certain untamed beauty about it, so different to what I was used to. If there was the luxury of time, I may have stopped to marvel at it all.

A shout came and the army slowly returned to its progress. There were a few murmurs of protest from the younger boys. I had been with them long enough to recognize the look of discontent. No doubt they wanted to split up and make their own way to Voinjama. Tiger King needed to keep his militia together or he would never be able to raise so many guns again. It wouldn't have surprised me to find a few of the younger members slipping out through the night. I patted Kyle on the shoulder and he zipped his bag up.

"What the hell are you looking for?" I asked, ready to be off.

"Nothing. I've lost something, that's all."

"Is it important?"

"Nah, buddy. Just forget it. Shall we?" He swept a hand in front, indicating I should go first.

"We'll go together." I pushed him along, and he laughed.

Kyle's mood had improved since we'd gotten clear of Zorzor. The fact that our pursuers could be close behind us didn't seem to faze him. Perhaps it was because we were heading in the right direction or that I was there, step-for-step with him, that he endured so well.

We passed some fallen trees, knotted together with vines and jungle detritus. The LURD hacked a space wide enough for us to go through two at a time. Had I more time, I would have attempted to camouflage where they hacked away. Instead, we passed through, the need for speed prevailing against caution.

The march was tough, nowhere was there level ground. Every step was a potential ankle-snapping endeavour. The humid air and rain added to the overall dreadfulness. It became a battle, man against the jungle. We were losing. Kyle began to flag, what little skin of his face that was visible had gone a sickly pale. His breathing was loud and rapid. Twice I had to stop with him for a few seconds of respite and so he could take on a little water. I took his other bag, just to lighten his load. He couldn't even say thanks, he just nodded and carried on. We weren't the only ones to lose pace with the rest. The few old men of The Bloody Hand Boys had fallen behind us. The column was staggered. We passed one young boy who simply lay at the side of the trail. Whether he collapsed from exhaustion, or merely snapped, I never did stop to discover. Kyle somehow still had his small digital camera out and filmed.

We continued on for another few hours, time seemed to distort. My feet were burning inside a marsh of socks. Blood from the blisters and sores washed about inside my boots. In the confusion of the attack, I'd neglected to put on my sturdy boots, instead wearing my 'comfort' footwear. There would be no relief for them, not until we came to the river would I get a chance to wash them, to let the rushing water soothe them, even for a moment.

Tiger King's voice cut through the jungle sounds, calling for a halt. Kyle and I had to walk another few minutes to reach where they were stopped. It was a tiny ravine, devoid of major foliage. Everyone would be pressed together, but nobody seemed to mind. Kyle collapsed to the first empty space he could find. I joined him. Tiger King stood watching me for a moment, his dark eyes fixed on my own. He looked as fresh as he would have if he had just woken up. A boy walked over to him and handed him a container of water. He raised it up over his head and let the contents fall over him. I'm not sure but I thought he smiled at me, if only for a second. The rest of The Bloody Hand Boys watched him waste the water. There was no doubt, Tiger King was in control.

I slumped down next to Kyle. There were roots and rocks littering the ground, it wasn't comfortable but it was better than standing. I used my pack as a pillow and stretched out my legs; they throbbed and my feet burned. I took some water from my canteen, it was warm but welcome. Kyle, again, rummaged through one of his bags, starting to swear under his breath.

"What the hell are you looking for? That's the second time that you've had your nose in that bag."

"It's silly, really. I thought I had something in here, I was saving it for an emergency. Holy shit, I found it."

Kyle pulled out a misshapen and filth-covered Mars Bar. He held it above his head in triumph. He smiled at me, cradling the chocolate. "I thought I'd lost it back in Zorzor." He peeled back the wrapper and inhaled. "That smells insanely good." It was halfway to his mouth and he paused. "You want some?" he asked, wiggling the melting chocolate at me.

As much as I would have loved to taste chocolate, my stomach was in constant discomfort. I probably could have used the sugar but I just couldn't face it. "No thanks, you knock yourself out."

Kyle shrugged and started to wolf down the chocolate bar. Among our camp, little fires were springing up. Not smart, and if Tiger King and I had not had that earlier altercation, I would have warned him against calling attention to ourselves. But I said nothing. Cassava rice was being prepared by those who brought it with them. Those who didn't would go hungry.

"Are those fires a good idea?" asked Kyle, chewing through the last of his treat.

"No. It's easy for the government men to follow our trail as it is. With those fires, a blind man could find us by smell alone."

"So what's next?" Kyle threw the wrapper into the undergrowth. Something about that bothered me. I harboured no special love for the jungle of Liberia, but his flippant disregard irked me.

"Have something to eat and then go to sleep. Tomorrow will be tough. I expect we'll arrive at the river. That could slow us down some. Anyway, don't worry about it. We'll find a way to get through. It's not that fast or deep," I lied.

"You're not worried?" Kyle shifted, stretching out on the ground.

"I'll be less worried when we put the river behind us. We lingered too long on the trail."

"You think they're after us already?"

I nodded. "The government commander can't let us escape to fight another day. They'll be after us. They'll only loot Zorzor for so long. We're moving slower because of the baggage. We need to pick up the pace tomorrow."

Kyle wiped his eyes with his thumb. "I feel like I could sleep for a year."

"Four hours," I warned. "Five at most. You want some rice?"

Kyle shook his head. "The chocolate's more than enough for me, buddy. Don't think I could face more of that gloop."

I pulled my pack open, inside I had a sealed plastic bag filled with cooked rice. I pulled out a handful, ignoring the filth on my hands. I pushed the lot into my mouth, followed by a quick gulp of water from the canteen. It tasted of nothing, turning into a bland paste in my mouth. I chewed a couple of times and choked it down. I'd gotten used to this way of eating. The lump of the stuff pushed its way down to my stomach. It settled with an uncomfortable feeling that would nevertheless keep hunger at bay.

"You should have some," I instructed Kyle.

He looked dubious, an eyebrow raised. "Gimme half of what you had, buddy."

I handed it over. Kyle attempted to mimic my technique but failed. He retched a few times and chewed furiously until finally he was able to swallow.

"Holy hell that was freaking terrible."

"I know. You get used to it, though."

"I hope not."

I unhooked my rifle, laying it next to me. Unzipping my tac vest, I let the burden off my shoulders and back. It felt good to have the weight off, if only for a few hours. I didn't trust the sentries that Tiger King would post. They would probably be asleep before me. I pulled my Glock from the holster, keeping it in hand. I settled down to sleep. It was impossible not to worry about sleeping on the jungle floor. There were all sorts of poisonous nasties that could crawl into camp and become an unpleasant bed mate. Kyle pulled out a thin blanket which he threw out over himself. It wasn't cold right now, but the nights could be deceptively chilly. If needed, we could all bunch up to share warmth.

"Hey, Mark?"

"Yes, Kyle."

He turned to me, propped up on one elbow. "Thanks for everything." He paused, looking up at the sky, and almost to himself he said, "Goodnight. Hope we see the morning."

I turned to look at the sentry, a boy of fifteen or so. He stood smoking, looking back into camp rather than in the direction we had come. I silently hoped that we would see the morning, too.

Chapter Five

The gentle whisper of hushed voices woke me. My heart thundered in my chest as I wiped at my eyes. Most of the camp was quiet, only a few fighters stirred. The fires were reduced to embers, the chocking smoke hung heavy in the ravine, catching in my throat. I coughed, raw and racking, and spat off to my right a few feet away from Kyle. He still slept, his face contorted with a look of concentration. Beneath the dried mud, his forehead creased and his mouth pinched. I stood and stretched. My back ached from the night on the jungle floor. At least this newest pain dulled the others which plagued me. The sentries were all asleep. It wasn't a huge surprise. If Tiger King or one of his lieutenants caught them, they would be in for a severe beating.

I checked my watch, we were an hour behind the time I wanted to be back on the trail. The anchoring fatigue refused to let me go, but we needed to move and soon. I stepped over to Kyle and used the toe of my boot to nudge him awake. His eyes slowly opened and looking about a moment, they finally settled on me.

"Time to get up," I said.

"Already?"

I nodded. He wiped his face with the palms of his hands. The dried mud flaked off, left his face more or less clean. He stretched, then stood. Yawning, he looked about the camp. Overnight, the dark circles below his eyes reached a purer shade of black.

"Drink something. Not too much, a few mouthfuls. You'll need the rest for the afternoon," I said.

Kyle nodded. Stooping down to retrieve his camera, he filmed the restful camp.

"I'm going for a piss."

I stepped over my things and started toward the latrine trench. As I passed, I nudged each sleeping form with my foot. I couldn't risk waking Tiger King myself but hopefully I started a chain reaction that would reach him.

The smell from the latrine was terrible, and the climate only made the stench worse. For one night an impossible amount of shit lay in the tiny ditch. I covered my mouth and nose with one hand, while unzipping with the other. Countless flies danced about over the pit. A young rebel, wearing a filthy white shirt, clinging to his thin frame joined me at the latrine. He pulled down his loose combat trousers and squatted down. I turned away and finished pissing. We were all used to the privations that soldiers endured.

My stomach gave a painful rumble and burning stitches followed, scorching down my right side. I clenched my teeth, tried to soothe the pain with my hand. It didn't help. Just after the young rebel went back to camp I knew that I was about to shit my guts out. I pulled down my trousers and straddled the rocks that encircled the trench. It came hard and fast and left me feeling weaker when I was finished. Improvisation in the jungle is key to surviving. Nobody, except Kyle, would consider packing toilet roll. I spotted a large leafed plant not far away. With the waist of my trousers in my hands I stepped off the rock and shuffled over to it. Pulling off a couple of the largest, cleanest looking leaves, I inspected them for bugs. Clear. Splashing a little water over them from my canteen I cleaned myself as best I could. At that moment I felt wretched, unclean and about ready to drop. But that wasn't an option.

I pulled myself together, sorted my trousers, and returned to camp. I met two LURD heading to the trench. They spoke quietly together, both carrying their weapons. Too late, I realised my lapse in judgement. I ran to camp, and to my things. Everything was where I left it. Kyle still filmed, one hand holding the camera, the other clutching his canteen.

I pulled on my tac vest and strapped the AK to it. I checked my Glock, secured in its holster. I made sure to never move more than a few feet from my weapons. I packed up the rest of my gear. A little way off, I heard Tiger King shouting, getting his forces ready. We would be moving out soon, still an hour behind schedule. My backpack felt just a little heavier today, my strength slowly being sucked from me by Liberia.

"Have you had water?" I called out to Kyle.

He nodded and swung the camera over to me. I ignored the attention of the lens, decided to check out positioning with the GPS. I pulled open the Velcro covering the pocket. Empty. The pocket next to it was the same. The satellite phone was missing also. I swore, and then swore again. Kyle, with a look of uncertainty, lowered the camera from me.

"What's wrong?"

"Has anyone touched my stuff since I've been away?"

"I dunno, I was filming the camp. What's missing?"

"The GPS and my satellite phone. Some little shit has probably taken it to sell later."

I had my suspicions where the phone and GPS went but I didn't want to panic Kyle. It wouldn't come as a surprise if I discovered that Tiger King somehow acquired the devices. Things were getting worse, it seemed like every little thing conspired against me. We had to keep moving, despite not having a map or being able to contact the outside world. There were many in our column who knew this area well enough so we wouldn't deviate from the path to Voinjama too much.

Kyle closed the distance between us. "Are we fucked?"

"Not yet. Once we put the river behind us, it'll be a little easier. We better get going."

Our camp site had emptied, Kyle and I were the only ones left in the ravine. He turned to me, his eyes twinkling with moisture. "I'm not cut out for this shit."

"Kyle—"

"I would get in, film some fighting, and get out without breaking a sweat. If I thought something like this would happen …"

"Kyle," I said, putting a hand on his shoulder. "I know you're scared, we all are, but we have to keep moving. It'll be worse if we just give up here and wait for the government forces to catch us. They won't care that you have connections back in the US. You're an enemy like me and all of the LURD. We have to move out. Now."

A few tears escaped, but he nodded, wiping them with the back of his hand. I gave his shoulder a reassuring squeeze and picked up the heaviest bag.

"You can do this."

I smiled to him and he returned the gesture. His was thin, and full of doubt, but at least he started moving. We walked through the remains of the camp, making a quick scan for anything of use that may have been left behind. There was nothing. We paused for a moment at the threshold of the jungle.

The heat was increasing by the minute.

I gave Kyle an encouraging nudge and he stepped into the foliage. I didn't blame him for being scared. I was scared but I had been in similar situations before. The fear didn't go completely, but it was suppressed now. Sweat already formed on my brow. Behind me, I scanned the far end of the ravine, imagining the massed guns of the government army. How much longer would our luck hold? They couldn't be too far behind in their pursuit. Had I the proper equipment, I could have rigged a few booby-traps, anti-personnel mines and the like, slowed their search down a little. I shook my head and stepped after Kyle. Back into the unknown of Liberia. More alone than ever.

Chapter Six

We arrived at the river a few hours later. The formidable barrier blocked our path. Kyle stood on the bank, snapping a few pictures. A local boy, familiar with the terrain searched for a crossing. I sat on a sharp boulder, covered in a spongy moss, slapping away the bugs that pestered me. It felt good to be out of the jungle, if only for a while. I was considering dunking my feet in the shallows, when the boy returned. A small bridge, unguarded, forded the river. Clear of government forces for the moment, Tiger King seized the opportunity and ordered everyone up and to the bridge.

"Looks like lady luck is paying us a visit today," muttered Kyle.

We followed the soldiers to the bridge. It was a dilapidated, and rotten wooden bridge, built years ago and forgotten, it stood as a reminder of a time before war tore Liberia apart. Kyle and I were two of the last to cross.

"What's the name of this river again, buddy?"

"Can't remember." Without my map I found it difficult to remember exactly.

Kyle slung one of his bags over his shoulder, freeing up a hand. He flipped off the flowing water beneath us. "Fuck you, river. Fuck you."

The wooden planking creaked at our passage, reminding us of the potential for disaster. I quickened my pace. Kyle rearranged his baggage and kept step with me. We reached the other side, unscathed. Behind, over the rushing of the water, we heard planks cracking, braking, and the curse as a soldier fell into the water. The current stole him before any thought of rescue could be mounted.

"Come on, Kyle," I said, trying to pull his attention from the drowned man. "We need to keep going."
Kyle watched a moment longer, then nodded. He closed his camera. "It was nice to be out in the open. Even for a little while."

Chapter Seven

The next eight days passed in a hazy nightmare. A rule of the march fell over us. When we moved through the undergrowth, neither of us spoke. It was only on our brief rest periods that we exchanged a few words. No matter what I said, nothing brought him out of his depression. To be honest, I didn't blame him. My knees and legs bled in a half dozen places from where I fell on unseen obstacles. The rocks concealed beneath the brush cut like razors. Not wanting to waste the few medical resources I had left, the wounds went untreated. I just limped on, cursing the blistering pain with every burning step.

We came to what I took to be as the Lawa river. We enjoyed a little time to pause on the banks while Tiger King sent out a few fighters to find a shallow part of the river for us to wade across. I thought it might take a while for them to find the crossing and I intended to soak my feet in the water. Kyle stood at its edge, threw a few rocks into the river. I was halfway through untying my laces when a LURD fighter, up to his waist in the fast flowing water, shouted and waved. They found a path and began crossing almost immediately. It was probably better I didn't see my feet, the sight of them would have probably sent me into a similar depression.

I turned to Kyle. He had his camera out filming the crossing, his face expressionless. It had become a matter of course for Kyle. He would film events because it was the only thing he could do.

"You should put anything electrical in one bag and keep it above your head when we cross."

Kyle nodded. "We're not going to suddenly hit a trench out in the middle of the water are we?"

"I hope not," I said, looking out into the river. "They seem to be crossing alright so far."

A single line of LURD waded through the water, their weapons and sensitive baggage held above the waterline. The river flowed quickly, but not enough to sweep a determined crosser from his feet. Those with a heavier burden shouted to others for aid. Above all else, the ammunition had to be kept dry.

I prepared my own backpack for crossing, placing anything that could be damaged inside. I strapped my AK to the top. Kyle adjusted his belongings, took my advice and placed all of the sensitive electrical equipment in one holdall. We stepped to the line waiting to cross. I watched more than one LURD slip and disappear under. They always appeared a few feet away, spitting water, sometimes with their burdens but more often than not, without. The line before us quickly diminished as the last of the rebels waded into the river. I wished someone had the foresight to take some rope. A strong swimmer could have went across the river and secured the line to a tree, giving us something to hold onto as we crossed. But it was just one of the many things I wished for in Liberia. There was little time to dwell on it as Kyle and I stepped in. Surprisingly, it was cool and for a moment, soothed my feet. The pain soon returned as I got deeper in the water. Kyle kept step with me. We moved slowly, testing each step before trusting our full weight to it. The water reached to my waist, with such force it caused me to stumble. There was nothing else to do but push on.

Kyle lagged behind. Where my steps were tentative, his were clumsy. His eyes, wide and wild, beckoned me to help him. He stretched out a hand toward me, like a child waiting for the reassuring touch of a parent. I waited for him to catch up, reaching out a hand which he grasped. I pulled him toward me.

"Don't go ahead of me again, please."

I nodded, and we continued on. I should have made Kyle stand directly behind me. What happened next was entirely my fault. Fatigue and a thousand other problems forced my desire to keep Kyle safe from the forefront of my mind. Kyle slipped, fell to the side, his feet swept by the flowing water. Disappearing from view, his backpack drifted away from him. I balanced my pack on top of my head and my free hand snatched at the straps of his bag. Somehow I managed to reach it. I pulled it to me and rested it on my back. Again I plunged my free hand into the water, feeling for Kyle. I couldn't see anything beneath the water. The reflection from the sun and the murkiness of the water prevented this. I can't remember how long Kyle was under; probably only eight to ten seconds but it felt longer. Had he been swept away? I shouted out his name as my hand frantically searched beneath the water. Kyle couldn't die. I wouldn't let him die. My hand finally touched his shirt. Grabbing at it, I pulled upwards. It felt like I was pulling him from a bog. He seemed stuck under the water before coming free. He broke the surface, sputtering water from his mouth. I pulled him close, putting my arm around him for support. He blew his nose and coughed.

"Don't … don't let me go."

I somehow managed to pull Kyle along. He didn't help me much, twice his feet went out from under him. He floated behind me, a dead weight, as I battled to bring us to safety. The height of the water fell and we stumbled onto the other bank, out of breath and thankful to have made it. Kyle collapsed down in the shallow water, there was a small rise on the bank to climb before we were truly safe. I urged him up and we forced our way over the riverbank. Now the both of us collapsed. Everything hurt, each breath burned in my chest. Pulling Kyle through the water sapped me of my last reserves of strength. The rebels were making camp. We should have been moving for another few hours but nobody had the will, or strength. A few little fires sprung up, with little care to clear the undergrowth from around them. Resting against the damp, I closed my eyes. I dozed for a while, I can't be sure how long but when I woke up, the light was fading. Kyle was fast asleep next to me, he hadn't stirred either. More fires dotted the camp, there was a faint smell of roasting meat. It was enough to motivate me to my feet.

My clothes clung to me, weighing me down. I dropped my pack and Kyle's, and went to gather some scrub to burn. There was plenty of debris dotted about the camp, enough for a small fire anyway. I piled it all on a clear patch on the ground, near to Kyle. We should have pushed on, put a little distance between us and the river. I gazed over the river, it was impossible for me to forget that the enemy could be a few hours away. As much as I wanted to move, nobody, including me, was able to continue on. We were hindered by fatigue.

The tone of the conversation I caught around camp had changed. Now that we passed the second river, there was hope that we escaped the pursuing government forces. I knew not to become caught up in the burgeoning optimism. Maybe we had, but I wasn't convinced, I wouldn't be until we were sitting in Voinjama. At the nearest fire six fighters sat. Two smoked and spoke in hushed voices, while the others slept. One of the smokers flashed a smile at me, the first one I'd seen in what felt like a lifetime. His front teeth were missing, I recognised his face but couldn't recall his name. He reminded me of the boy that Tiger King had beaten. The strange thing was, now I couldn't remember the face of the boy. All I could recall were his injuries, the mewing sounds he made. When he raised a hand, begged me to stay before I left him to die. Maybe it was because it was easier not to remember individuals in war.

"We safe now, Mak."

The way he said it, I couldn't tell if it was a question or a statement. "It won't be long until we're in Voinjama."

He leaned back against a tree trunk and took a long draw on his smoke. I knelt down, pulled a burning stick from the fire. Shielding the flame with my hand, I returned to Kyle and ignited our own. I nursed it until I was sure it wasn't going to go out. Kyle stirred and opened his eyes, wiped down his face and yawned.

Searching around the clearing, he asked, "We're alright?"

"For now. You should come here and dry off your clothes. You'll feel better for it."

Kyle scrambled over on his hands and knees and began pulling off his shirt. There was still heat but it would soon disappear as night swallowed us up. Kyle removed his boots and began to remove the rest of his clothes.

"You should check your camera bag. It got soaked in the river."

He pulled the bag over to the fire, began searching through his belongings. I pulled off my own clothes until I stood in my underwear. There was nowhere to hang them so I just wrung them out as best I could and laid them by the fire. My feet were in agony and I wanted to take a little time to just soak them in the river. It was almost sickening to look at them. They were covered in cuts, several dark bruises marked the skin. On my left foot there was a patch of pure white, almost ulcerated skin. It wouldn't surprise me if I ended up with a limp. My feet were truly in a horrible condition, constantly throbbing.

I hobbled over to the riverbank, each step like walking on fire. When I reached the bank, I slid down on my side and crawled over to the water. Stretching my legs out, I pushed my feet in. I almost cried out in a mixture of relief and pain. Sitting there, somehow a little hope managed to work its way back to me. The sound of the flowing river before me and the sounds of the jungle behind, actually relaxed me a little. It could have been enjoyable under different circumstances.

I stayed there for a while, almost dropping off once or twice. There were hundreds of stones littering the riverbank. I picked up a handful and threw them, one by one, into the water. As the last one left my hand, a small light flickering on the other side of the river caught my eye. I had been here before, mistaking the occupants of the jungle for something more sinister. The dark made it impossible to see exactly what flickered. It looked like a reflection off metal, or possibly a small flashlight. I told myself to ignore it and head back to Kyle and the camp. And almost did. Except I heard a voice. I pulled my feet from the river and stayed low. On hands and knees, I crawled back to the riverbank, ignoring the fresh cuts that the rocks inflicted. At the top of the bank, I called out to Kyle.

"What?"

"Do any of your cameras have night vision mode?" I asked, my voice little more than a whisper.

"Yeah, it sucks, though. You can't see shit through it."

"Doesn't matter, pass it over here, keep your head down."

"Why?" asked Kyle, uncertainty lacing his voice.

"Just pass me the camera and stay down. Pass me my gun, too."

Kyle emerged from the camp, sliding along on his knees, the camera and my AK clutched to his chest. I placed a finger to my lips, motioning for silence. Kyle handed me the camera and gun. I waved him down low. He disappeared, I could just make him out moving back to camp and our fire. The camera was already set on night vision mode, the screen illuminated in a dirty green. I slipped the strap over my neck, silently thanking Kyle for pre-setting it for me. I cocked the AK gently, and slid back to the edge of the river. I couldn't make anything out on the opposite riverbank now. The sound was only of the flowing water and the faint hint of our camp behind me. I held the camera up to my face. Kyle was right, the night vision sucked. The screen was filled with green, the river only slightly visible. I should have asked him how to zoom the focus. I pressed a few button but nothing helped. Somehow, the way I held the camera, my finger brushed the trigger and the camera flash burst out over the river. The reply was instant. I saw the muzzle flashes before I heard the snap of the shots. I threw myself back from the river. They were firing blind, but they must have known the general direction where I was. More than a few rounds impacted around me, throwing up clumps of ruddy sand. I clawed my way up and over the riverbank, fell face first to safety. LURD fighters were running toward me, all armed and shouting.

"Kill the fires," I shouted. Nobody listened. The faint glow from our campfire would have been enough for the enemy to spot a head held a little too high. I snapped my AK stock down and held it ready. Kyle was next to me. More fighters were throwing themselves onto the riverbank and firing their weapons.

"Hold your fire! Save your ammo!" Again, nobody listened. Tiger King was somewhere, ordering his soldiers to shoot.

"The government?" Kyle shouted to be heard. He pulled the camera from around my neck.

"Yes!"

"We're fucked!"

"They can't cross while we hold this side of the river."

Kyle nodded and put his camera over the top of the bank. All he would be able to film would be muzzle flashes and tracer fire. I again shouted for the rebels to cease fire.

Some held their fire, but the blind fire fight went on for another ten minutes. An uneasy calm settled. Again, the only sound was the river. A few voices questioned who we were shooting at, but they were ignored.

Kyle snapped closed his camera. "So, what happens now?"

"We wait for tomorrow," I said, chancing a glance over the bank.

"Then what?"

"Then we figure out this problem. We can't retreat from here without leaving a force to protect our rear. They would just cross and it would be a very short battle for us. We can't stay here indefinitely or it will become a siege. We would run out of supplies and possibly be encircled. It would be game over. Get some sleep, Kyle. We'll figure it out tomorrow."

"You expect me to be able to sleep after that? My heart is going like a dammed jackhammer."

"You should try." I stood, but stayed crouched. "You'll need the rest for tomorrow," I whispered. I went back to our fire and dressed. The clothes were still wet but it was getting colder. I threw a handful of chipped wood onto the small flames. They sparked and spat while I settled down for a few hours of much needed sleep. Tomorrow, a terrible decision would have to be made. Who would stay behind to stall the government forces long enough for us to get away?

Chapter Eight

Gunfire, my constant companion throughout the night. Even in my turbulent dreams, I fought imaginary battles. Perhaps, ones yet to be fought. Reduced to only a smouldering pile, the fire produced little light or warmth. A young fighter slept beside me, snoring loudly. Kyle lay on his back, an arm draped over his face. If we were going to make it out of the jungle, Kyle had to play his part. Since leaving Zorzor he had become an additional burden.

Reaching over, I took hold of his foot and gave it a couple of shakes. "Kyle? You awake?"

A pained groan came from him. "No."

"We need to talk."

"Can't it wait until morning, Mark?"

"No."

He sat up, scratching his arm. It was hard to make out his facial expression in the dim light, but I guessed he was pissed at me.

"What is it? It's not imminent death, so speak."

I couldn't rationalise what I wanted to say without it sounding like a pep-talk or patronising. I let out a sigh. A half-burnt stick hung from the edge of the fire. I picked it up and prodded the ashes and embers. I kept my eyes fixed on the fire. "I need you to help me."

"How? What can I do? I shouldn't even be out in this shitty jungle."

"You shouldn't be here?" I held the stick out before me, like a weapon. "Then what the fuck are you doing in Liberia? You think you're the only one who's had a shit turn of luck? Do you? Take a look at yourself. You're not even trying to help yourself. You're letting me do everything. All you do is put one foot in front of the other. I need you to do more. I need you … not to be a burden." I shook my head.

In the gloom, Kyle's eyes shone bright. Whether I reduced him to tears, or it was a trick of the light, I don't know. I turned back to the fire and stabbed at it again. A painful silence fell between us. I was actually glad of the sporadic gunfire flying overhead, harmlessly filling the void between the two of us.

"You finished?" Kyle asked, devoid of emotion.

"Yes." I threw my stick into the fire and turned. He looked away. "I probably shouldn't have said that. It wasn't a kind thing to do."

"No, you said your peace. That's fine. I'm going back to sleep."

Kyle lay down and pulled his bags close, resting his head on one of them. He swept an arm over his face, covering his eyes. "Night, Mark."

I couldn't be sure, but I got the feeling that he was crying softly. I eased myself back, shifting around, unable to get comfortable. I lay, looking up at the sky.

I hated the times before sleep. My mind, unoccupied with the immediate need to stay alive, wandered. For some reason, I thought back to meeting Kyle for the first time, how he immediately assumed I was a mercenary. The other guys in the company had no problem labelling themselves that. With military backgrounds, years of service under their belts, they would have happily fought in the wars of others. Was I any different? Did I bury what I really was under the pretence of ideals and morals? Was I really just a man unwilling to serve in the regimented military, with a penchant for violence? Did I willingly profit from the pain and suffering of others? Questions and self-doubts like these always plagued me before sleep. I did what I could to suppress them for another time.

I rolled over to my side, away from the fire. Tomorrow would be the make or break day of our odyssey in the jungle. A small whisper in my mind told me to take

Kyle and slip away from the group, and make our own way back. If I still had my GPS, then perhaps, but now, we were relying on the knowledge of local trackers. If we ran into trouble, the guns of The Bloody Hand Boys would make the difference between a fighting chance and slaughter. We would stay with the group. I closed my eyes. This could be the last chance to sleep for the next few days. Somehow the lullaby of gunfire aided my slumber.

Chapter Nine

Kyle and I sat on a rocky outcropping, watching Tiger King among his troops. Flanked by two of his lieutenants, he occasionally touched a fighter on the head. Some of those he touched looked to each other, some of the younger ones held hands. The older fighters, kept their eyes down, not reacting to the touch. I sipped water from my canteen. Kyle and I devoured the last of the cassava rice upon waking. The rancid taste still lingered in my mouth.

"It's random," said Kyle, filming Tiger King. "Poor bastards."

"You think so?" There was still gunfire over the river. The light of the morning had yet to descend fully. Using my canteen, I pointed toward Tiger King. "Look who he is picking. Notice anything?" Kyle remained silent. Eventually he shook his head. "It's the old, the wounded, or those too weak to keep up. He's cutting away the dead flesh and throwing it to the dogs. It'll keep them at bay for a while."

"Shit," Kyle whispered. "Sucks to be them."

"We're lucky it wasn't us. Imagine what would have happened if he'd ordered us to stay."

"Then it would've sucked to be us." Kyle smiled, finding some gallows humour.

"Yep. Look, whatever happens today, don't draw attention to us. We'll linger near the back, keep out of Tiger King's sight. Things might get a little shitty as the day goes on."

"I'm getting used to each day sucking worse than the last." Kyle snapped closed the camera. "We'll have to move soon?"

I screwed the top onto my canteen, slipping it back onto my belt. "Yep, in the next few minutes I expect."

"Then I'm going for a piss."

"Good idea."

We both walked toward the latrine, skirting the edge of our camp. Walking in silence we watched the chosen men receive their weapons, an AK-47 for every second fighter. Only one magazine issued to each rifle. If they knew what that meant, nobody voiced their complaint. It was a simple choice, fight at the river and survive, or die for defying Tiger King. It was a shit choice, one I was glad we wouldn't need to make. Kyle filmed as Tiger King's lieutenants separated the chosen and forced them to the river to take over the fighting.

The latrine reeked worse than the day before. I would have just pissed in camp, but my guts churned, usually a prelude to horrendous diarrhoea. I tried to breathe through my mouth, but somehow the offending stench became lodged in my throat. I could almost taste it. Kyle coughed a few times. We stood side-by-side. I slipped my AK onto my back and unzipped. The scabies burned worse than normal. As I pulled myself free from my trousers, the metal zipper raked against me.

"Fuck!" I sucked in the feted air, my eyes flowing with water. It was a few moments before I could actually manage to piss.

Kyle heard. "What's up?"

"The scabies is worse than normal today. It's burning like a mother … hell."

Kyle winced in sympathy, looking down. He whistled low. "Jesus, buddy. I've never seen a dick look like that before."

"What? This big?"

"No, covered in that kind of … rash."

"Just be thankful it's not you." I finished pissing and, against my better judgement, checked myself. The rash seemed to have reached an even deeper, angrier red. It was hard to imagine it ever being normal again.

Kyle began laughing beside me, not softly, but almost uncontrollably. Such a foreign sound, for a second I couldn't make sense of it.

"Imagine if you brought a girl home one night, and you unzipped producing that monstrosity. Shit, she would run miles rather than let that thing near her."

I began to laugh, too. I couldn't stop it. Neither of us could. We stood there, dicks in hand, laughing at my pain. I didn't care. Like my tears days before, the emotions needed to come out. More importantly, Kyle was back. Whether it was my talk through the night, or just him accepting his situation, I didn't know. Our chances of surviving increased a fraction.

"You're a daft bastard, Kyle."

"And you're going to scare a lot of girls when we get out of here."

Chapter Ten

We moved out shortly after returning from the latrine.
There were more than a few tearful goodbyes between
those picked to stay and the rest of The Bloody Hand Boys.
One of those picked by Tiger King to stay, an older man
with a limp, made a run for the jungle. Tiger King shot him
twice in the head before he could run ten feet. Kyle's
camera captured the entire scene.

We marched away, back into the undergrowth. The
sound of gunfire soon grew faint. I carried one of Kyle's
bags. He kept pace with me, occasionally chatting as we
moved. We lingered at the rear of the columns. There was
an unspoken sense of urgency. Even those without any
tactical knowledge knew that the defenders left at the river
wouldn't last long. When they broke, the chase would be
joined. It would be closer than ever before.

The sounds of explosions came from behind. A few
of the fighters turned to look.

"Mortars," I said, before Kyle could ask. "Get
moving." I urged those who stopped onward.

I jogged the few feet until I was next to Kyle again.
Speaking softly, he leaned in closer to hear. "I think we
should move up the column a little. If they have mortars
up, Tiger Kings resistance will crumble. I thought they
could at least buy us a day or two."

"What about Tiger King?"

"We'll just stay out of his way, alright?"

Kyle nodded, the smile he had most of the day
disappeared.

We moved past the slower elements of the column.
Nobody paid much attention; they were too concerned with
their own problems.

The sounds of the mortars and gunfire ceased.
Either we moved too far into the undergrowth, or the battle
reached its inevitable conclusion. Tiger King allowed us

five minutes of respite before marching off again. He didn't look like he had even broken a sweat. He was built for war. Kyle again began his chatting. The conversation mindless, the type you have when trying to overcome the boredom of a tedious journey. I kept checking over my shoulder. Our column was staggered, those lagging behind no longer in sight. It wouldn't surprise me to find some who decided to take their chance alone in the jungle instead of slogging to Voinjama with us.

Chapter Eleven

The night came finally. We fell where we stood. No semblance of a camp, no fires or food. Only drinking some water and sleeping for a couple hours. It concerned me that there were no sentries, but no one could have fought off the fatigue to stand watch. I knew I couldn't. Thoughts of the potential danger raced through my mind. Even when I closed my eyes, my mind wouldn't shut off. Nevertheless, sleep came.

The crack of gunfire again, this time closer, much closer. The camp awakened, shifting to action. I pulled a sluggish Kyle to his feet, my AK in hand.

Wide-eyed, Kyle searched for the source of the sound. "Where is it?"

I slipped the stock of my AK out and cocked the weapon. "Close, too close. Does your camera use memory cards?"

He nodded. His camera was out, but not filming. Where I instinctively grabbed my weapon, Kyle seized his camera.

"Then I think it would be a good idea to take them out and ditch everything else."

"Are you crazy? You know how much everything costs?"

A round splintered a slim tree trunk next to us. Kyle fell to the ground and started pulling open his packs, ripping free the precious memory cards. I knelt, scanning for movement. It must have been some poor bastard slipping away running into our pursuers. Unlucky for them, but their death gave us a chance. Tiger King, holding his weapon in one hand, fired into the jungle. He stood, a rigid statue of defiance and death. I couldn't see who he was shooting at, if anyone. The rest of the fighters ran. One of Tiger King's lieutenants tried to halt the retreat, to hold them, get them to fight. He held up several fighters who milled around him for a moment, then he fell, clutching his chest. In the faint light, I saw a dull glint off the blade protruding from his chest.

"Right, we're leaving."

"Just a second, buddy."

We didn't have a second. Any resistance the fighters mounted was on the verge of collapse. They were running, their burdens of ammunition and water discarded. Tiger King emptied his magazine. Finding himself alone, he retreated, back into the jungle.

Crouched low, between two trees, I saw the first of our pursuers. With the stock to my shoulder, I squeezed off two rounds, close enough to Kyle that he covered his ears. The figure fell, clutching his right shoulder. I told myself I aimed to incapacitate him, but that was a lie.

"Shit, buddy. Don't fire that so close to my head."

I grabbed Kyle by the backpack, pulling him to his feet. "We've got to go."

"I just need to get …"

Our makeshift camp became a killing zone. A murderous volley of fire ripped through the cramped space. I threw Kyle down, seconds later falling myself, landing on top of him.

"Keep your fucking head down!"

Parts of trees and brush, shredded by the fire, fell about us, like a heavy downpour. Kyle screamed, no words, just noise. Hidden partially by the jungle floor, the rounds passed above us. Pushing the AK to my back, I pulled my Glock. It would be much more effective if it came to fighting here. It took a couple of seconds to target with the AK. My Glock gave me an advantage, a scant one, but I needed all the help I could get.

Chambering a round, I shouted into Kyle's ear, "Start crawling! That way!" I pointed with the pistol toward where the LURD fighters melted away. He continued to cry. I grabbed the back of his neck in a vice grip. He stopped. "Move that way or we both die. Move!"

He nodded, starting to crawl over the jungle floor. I followed close behind, every twenty seconds checking over my shoulder for danger. The adrenaline pushed us on, but the burning in my arms and legs felt like four demons pushing their red-hot pokers into my flesh. The crawl tore off all the scabs on my knees and arms, opening the healing wounds. That minor pain was lost in the myriad of others I endured.

Kyle halted. I couldn't hear what he said. I had to crawl over his back to get close enough to understand, but it was apparent why he stopped. A fighter, in his death throws, blocked our path. The man, young and shirtless gazed to the canopy above, his body convulsing violently.

What could we do? Cover was thin, and might reveal us to our ruthless enemy.

"Crawl over him."

"He's not dead, yet!"

"Do it, Kyle! Or it's us who'll be lying next to him."

"Jesus Christ!"

Kyle tentatively placed his arms over the body and pulled himself over. The dying man spat blood like a small fountain. I crawled up to him, the stench of blood and shit strong. "I'm sorry," I whispered. Before I could cross over him, his eyes became clear. They flickered to me, then just beyond, and narrowed, then stilled. Just like his body. Something about the look? I'd been forgetting my twenty second checks.

I turned, saw the AK pointed at me, and fired on instinct. The boy's face shattered like a broken jigsaw puzzle, blood and skull fragments blasting out the back of his head. He fell, his face smashing against my boot. Somehow, I managed to remain calm. I thanked the boy's hesitation. It saved my life. His AK fell next to me.

Grabbing it by the muzzle, I pulled it to me, removing the magazine. All the while, I prayed that nobody saw my Glock's muzzle flash. I stuffed the spare ammo into my vest pocket. I tried to ignore the age of the boy, the AK looked like an oversized toy in his arms. There would be a chance to dwell the next time I attempted to fall asleep. I hadn't the time for anymore reverence for the dead. I crawled over the corpse in front of me, the familiar stench of the dead stinging my senses. Kyle had kept going and was out of the clearing. I followed. Reaching him, my breath lost in the effort, I somehow managed to tell him to get up and run. He nodded grimly, his brow knitting. He didn't run.

He paused, helping me to my feet. "I can't do this without you."

Exhausted, my adrenaline all but gone, Kyle propped me up. I didn't look back. I didn't need to. A hail of rounds followed us, impacting off to our right. Together, we ran.

Chapter Twelve

We blundered around in the undergrowth, the sounds of battle trailing at our heels. At times, gunfire came from all around. I let go of Kyle, now able to walk on my own.

"What now?" Kyle wiped the sweat from his brow with the back of his hand. Breathing heavily, his eyes remained calm.

"Wait here for a moment. I need to think."

I leaned against a thick tree trunk. It was rough under my hand, the ridges in the bark sharp enough to cut should I have pulled away too fast.

"What do you think happened to Tiger King and his men?"

I shrugged. "Dead, maybe. Or running. They're still shooting, so there's a good chance some of the LURD are alive still."

"Do we need to meet up with them?"

I didn't have an answer. We needed The Bloody Hand Boys' guns. But two men could perhaps slip through the government lines should we now be behind them. It was a life or death choice to make. I looked to Kyle. He watched me, licking his lips expectantly. Kyle couldn't help me choose. He was a follower. I hated having to make the decision.

"I think now … it's better for us to try to make it on our own."

Kyle's eyes searched my face for a moment before he spoke. "Okay, Mark. Do you think it's best?"

"I do." I pulled my canteen from my belt. It was light. When I shook it, only a few mouthfuls tumbled inside. "You got much water left?"

Kyle fiddled with his camera. "Batteries almost dead. Shit. Water? Yeah, I've got about a quarter left. You want some now?"

"Save it."

The water wasn't an issue. Everything hinged on today.

"You should take a little now."

Kyle switched his camera off, letting it rest on the cord around his neck. He drank two mouthfuls. I drained my canteen, cursing the limited water. It felt like I had sand in my mouth. Even running my tongue over my teeth was unpleasant.

"So where now?"

"That way." I pointed ahead. The jungle seemed to thin in that direction. That could only be a good thing. Our progress would speed up, increasing our chances to outrun the government forces. "The jungle's opening up that way. Means we'll reach open ground soon enough. Voinjama, the next few days." *Unless we run into trouble.*

"We're going to make it, Mark. We've come this far. We have to make it."

"Of course we will. Just stay close to me. Do everything I say, and we'll get home."

"Alright, buddy," said Kyle with a resolute smile. "Lead on."

I took hold of my rifle, stepping over a few downed trees wrapped in thick, twisting vines. Behind me, I felt Kyle fall in.

We broke into a light jog. On more even ground our progress became easier. The gunfire, which never stopped, seemed more distant. Each time there was a crack of shooting, Kyle no longer flinched. The sounds filtering through the jungle were distorted. It was impossible to accurately judge distance or direction. I saw movement in my periphery. I brought my AK to the ready, only to lower it a second later. Creatures scurrying to escape our procession, nothing more sinister.

Kyle let his mouth run while we marched. At first, I hushed him, wanting to be alert to trouble. I soon realised his chat was just a way of coping with the hardship. I let him speak, half listening, always scanning ahead. Searching the shadows for peril.

"So what do you miss the most being out here?"

"I dunno."

"Come on, buddy. It helps me relax if we speak."

"Cheeseburgers. How about that?"

Kyle gave a gruff laugh. "Shit, we all miss proper food. And trust me, the burgers in England suck. You wait until you taste a proper American burger. You ever been to the States?"

"No." I halted, holding my hand up. A blast of heavy calibre gunfire ripped through the calm, off to our right. Kyle's hand rested on my shoulder.

"Are they close?" he whispered in my ear.

"Keep quiet." I dropped to my knees. "Keep low. And follow me." Kyle did the same, landing with a painful grunt.

I led Kyle off to the left, veering away from the sound as best I could. It grew fainter again. Within minutes, Kyle resumed chatting.

"I tell you what, buddy. When we get out of here, you need to come visit me. I'll show you a proper burger."

I couldn't think about what would happen if we escaped, or make promises to see Kyle in America. My mind resisted such thoughts. It had become rooted in the misery of Liberia.

"So what do you miss?" I asked, slapping a bug feasting on my neck.

"Me? I'll tell you what I miss, tits. Girls who take their clothes off for money," He laughed. "My cell phone, my apartment, my cat. Even my asshole neighbour, who plays shit music through the night. That's what I miss. You know? Normality."

"What's your cat's name?" I rolled the corpse of the bug between my thumb and forefinger, flinging it off into the foliage.

"Mysti, the untraditional spelling. Don't ask, she came with the name."

Before I could ask why, we came to a sharp rise in the terrain. I scaled the incline on hands and knees, razor-edged rocks hidden by greenery scraped at my skin. As I reached the summit, I peered over. Down a little hollow, two soldiers reloaded a PKM machine gun. The same type of machine gun that pinned us down at Zorzor. Unlike The Bloody Hand Boys, they wore DMP camouflage uniforms. I sank down, hugging the moist earth. Blindly, I reached behind, pushing Kyle back. I turned with my index finger to my lips. Thank God, he wasn't speaking as we climbed. He raised a hand, indicating he understood. Slowly, he crept up beside me. I tapped his forehead twice, then pointed down. He nodded once, his smile lacking humour.

Keeping low to the ground, he peered over, pulling back almost instantly. Shaking his head, he mouthed 'shit' three times. I pointed to my AK, trying to indicate they were enemies. Kyle shrugged, his eyes narrowing.

I pulled him back down the incline, controlling our descent, reducing the noise. I wasn't happy about speaking with government forces so close, but Kyle didn't understand my clumsy signing.

Whispering, I said, "Those two are government soldiers."

"Fuck me!" he said. "Are you sure?"

I waved away the question. "We need to take them out."

"Can't we go around them?"

I shook my head. "We can't leave the machine gun operational. If we somehow made it past them, it would shred our cover down in the gully."

"So what's the plan?"

I licked my cracked lips, tasting dirt and blood. I spat out the vile taste. Taking a deep breath, I told Kyle something I knew he didn't want to hear. "I need you to take one of them."

"Have you lost your fucking mind?" he replied, eyes wide. "Just shoot them."

It annoyed me, his flippant suggestion that I should kill them. Like I valued life any less than him.

"I can't. If I shoot them, others will hear it and we'll be dead. It needs to be done silently."

The machine gunners were probably situated in the rear. The rest of the government forces just a little ahead. Should they hear my shots, we would be dead within seconds. I pulled my combat knife from my belt. Many large stones littered the ground. I picked one, the size of a small melon and pushed it to Kyle. "All you have to do is hit him on the back of the head or neck. Make sure you mean it. You can't let him shout out or draw attention to this position."

"Mark, I can't." He shrank away from the rock like it would explode. "Can't we go back?"

"Kyle, you know we can't go back. We don't have the supplies, and there are probably more of them back that way. We need to get to Voinjama. If you want to survive you need to do this."

"Give me the Glock. Maybe I can do it with the pistol."

"I can't do that. If you shoot and miss, we're dead. If you shoot and the others hear, we're dead. It has to be done silently."

Kyle wiped at his face. "I can't. I know you need me, but I just can't. I'm not a soldier."

I tried to ease him with a smile. "I know you're not. You just need to do this one thing, then we'll get you back home, okay?"

"Can't you do them both?"

"If I miss, or one gets a shot off or shouts out, we're dead. It has to be done at the same time. I know what you're feeling, really I do. I'd never killed anyone before I met you. This is as close to murder as you'll ever get, but you're doing it to survive. Blame me if it makes it easier, but you have to do this. You have to take him out."

Kyle clamped a hand over his mouth, looking like he was about to throw up. He rocked back and forth, eyes fixed on the rock at his feet. He kept repeating, "I can't."

"Kyle." He ignored me. "Kyle." I seized his face in my hands, forcing his eyes onto me. "If you want to live, you'll do this." I pushed the rock into his hands. "We need to do this now."

"Can't … can't I just knock him unconscious?"

"We can't take the chance. What if he wakes up before we make it clear? You know what we have to do."

He looked at the rock as if something alien. I pushed him with enough force that he began climbing up the incline. I joined him, matching his movement. We snaked up, reaching the top, and paused. I motioned for silence. The two soldiers beneath us sat smoking, speaking to one another. The rake of gunfire came from down beyond the gully. That was where we needed to go. Off to my right, a small congregation of government soldiers descended into the gully. I prayed they wouldn't look back.

My combat knife felt heavy in my hands. Could I really end a man's life with it? I'd only used it for peeling the occasional fruit or, in moments of boredom, whittling sticks. How best to kill with a knife? I'd never thought I'd have to contemplate such a thing. It was barbaric in practice. Battles should be fought with guns, not blades. In the movies, it was by slitting the throat. Stabbing the heart had a greater chance of missing. How could I compare the movies to actually taking someone's life?

I nodded to Kyle, helping him over the lip of the incline. With careful movement, we crept down. There wasn't much loose detritus for us to dislodge. We reached the bottom. Kyle would take the sitting soldier on the right, me the standing soldier on the left. Five feet away, I reversed the knife so the cutting edge was toward me. Four feet, I stepped over a tangle of broken vines. Three feet, a glance to Kyle. Two feet, he shook his head, face deathly pale. I nodded.

When I saw Kyle swing the rock over arm, I reached for the mouth of the standing soldier. I clamped my hand over it. No stubble greeted my hand, his youthful face smooth. I thrust the combat knife over this throat, pulling his head back. I slashed the blade across. There was little resistance. The blood sprayed out as we collapsed backwards. The weight of the dying soldier blasted the air from me. Gasping, I looked over to see Kyle slamming the rock repeatedly down on the fallen man. The solder raised his arms, warding off the assault. Kyle's kept his eyes closed as he brought the rock down. The initial strike must have rendered the soldier unable to shout out, or he surely would be crying in pain. I threw the dying man off me. His hands went to his throat, eyes wide. He looked wildly about, unable to stop his lifeblood pumping out. I got to my feet, kicked Kyle off the dying soldier. Straddling him, I stabbed down once into his shoulder. The second strike to the middle of his chest. His arms still fought me. The third caught his forearm, stripping skin and muscle away, revealing the pale bone beneath. The skin flapped like a wet flag. His face distorted, almost inhumanly as he grasped at his flayed limb. Blood washed over the both of us. The vile taste was in my mouth.

"Just fucking die!"

The last thrust went deep into the left ribs. The blade refused to come free. I fell back, the thrashing of the soldier finally subsided. I could hear Kyle crying. Covered in two men's blood, I lay there, wanting nothing more than to close my eyes and not wake up. I couldn't. I looked up to see Kyle puking. There was no time to be tender. We had a chance and needed to take it.

I stood. "Get up. Put the camo jacket on." I used my AK to point at the dead soldier. Removing my backpack, I pulled the second soldier's blood-stained jacket free. "Put the fucking jacket on, Kyle."

Kyle wiped his mouth, pulled the jacket off the corpse, and put it on. He threw up again. I searched through my bag for the essentials. The medical kit, I attached to my tac vest. Everything else I abandoned. The less weight the better. I left the backpack there, next to the two dead soldiers. Kyle only carried his camera as baggage. He wasn't filming.

"What's the matter? Your own handy work not good enough to be filmed?" I pointed to the corpse. Kyle looked down, his face streaked with blood. I was angry, raging at the only available target. It was Liberia and the war I truly hated. I needed to calm down. It wasn't his fault. "I'm sorry, Kyle." I swallowed down the chocking bile. "It's not you. It's this fucking place. This God damned war."

He looked at me, his brow knotted. "I understand …" It seemed like he wanted to say more but he just repeated himself. "I understand." His voice shook, timid and hollow.

"Come on." I gripped him hard on the shoulder. "We can make it through their lines."

I pointed down the gully. We would ditch the camo jackets once we got clear. If The Bloody Hand Boys were still fighting, they might mistake us for government forces.

Taking Kyle by the arm, we began our perilous descent, painfully slow.

Chapter Thirteen

After escaping the gulley we became bogged in a game of
evading passing elements of the government army. We
shadowed the thin road that cut through the jungle, keeping
far enough away from the red-sand road to avoid detection,
but close enough to not become lost. As the sky darkened,
we found the imposing barrier of the Lofa river. Kyle and I
hunkered down against sharp rocks and scraping vines,
exhausted.

Kyle scrambled up next to me and peered over our
shelter. "That's one big ass river."

"I know," I said, loosening my tac vest and rubbing
a shoulder.

Kyle slid back. "Guess we can't try and swim it?"

I shook my head, pulling a sharp vine off my arm.
"I wouldn't advise it. I can hardly walk, let alone swim."

"So what now?"

Sitting by the river was a welcome respite. For once
in as long as I could remember, no gunfire. No severe
voices. Nobody trying to kill us. Kyle and I could have
been alone, swallowed up by the Liberian jungle but I
knew we weren't. All around us, government forces
swarmed the jungle like locusts, seeking to destroy the last
remnants of the LURD rebels, and us.

"We need to get across," I said, scratching an old
scratch on my elbow.

"But how?" asked Kyle, his eyes closed, a slight
grimace playing across his face.

I released a sigh. "There's got to be a bridge
somewhere close by." I pointed off to my right.
"Somewhere over there."

Kyle opened his eyes. "How can you even know
that?"

"The road we were ghosting, it's got to lead
somewhere. Besides, we've seen enough government

troops to think they're heading to Voinjama in force. I doubt they would all cross at one section, too risky. There's got to be a bridge nearby." Even as the words left my mouth, I wondered how much of my logic was created from hope and desperation.

Kyle seemed to mull over my reply, chewing his cracked lips. "If what you say is true, Mark, how are two white guys going to manage to cross a bridge? It's probably guarded by government soldiers. Like you said in the gulley, you can't risk shooting otherwise it'll draw attention to us."

"Have an hour to rest, Kyle. I'll think of something."

"I hope so." Kyle stretched out, muttering as he stifled a yawn.

It wasn't long before he was asleep, little grunts coming each time he took a breath. I dared not risk sleep. Too many dangers lurking around us. I listened to the flow of the river, desperately seeking an answer to the bridge problem. Nothing came to mind. Thoughts dulled, and I could feel the crushing weight of fatigue capture me. I struggled for a moment, forcing my eyes open. It didn't work. I must have dozed. The night was total when I opened my eyes. Kyle was beside me, his breathing deep and far too loud in the dark. I sat bolt upright, cursing myself for the danger I'd put us both in. I scrambled over to him, shaking his foot.

Kyle woke with a grunt, a frantic hand flapping at me

"Relax, Kyle," I said. "It's me."

"You trying to make me shit myself? I thought it was them."

"Shut up," I said, letting go of his foot. "You were snoring too loud."

Kyle sat up, pulling his legs in, his knees up to his chin. "You heard something out there?" he asked, pulling a hand over his face.

The truth was I heard nothing, and my scalding of Kyle was more to do with the fact I'd left us in danger. "I don't know, there's a lot of movement out there. I can't tell if it's the sound of the jungle or worse.

We stayed quiet for a time, the sounds of the jungle alive around us. There wasn't much to be said. At present we were fucked, if only literally stuck on the wrong side of the river, probably surrounded. Food was a problem and nothing I thought of to get us across the water seemed likely to work. It came down to two possible solutions, swim the perilous river or fight our way across. I wasn't sure which was more foolish, or more dangerous. Both would probably result in the same. Our deaths.

Off to the right, a strange sucking sounded, as if someone pulled a stick from mud.

"Shit!" Kyle jerked his hand upward. "Stuck my hand in a shitty mud puddle." He brought it to his face and sniffed. "Stinks like hell," he said, pulling his hand away.

"Can't see shit out here," I told him. "If that was your foot that went in there, you'd probably have snapped your ankle."

"Wait!" said Kyle, his unexpected cry had me bringing my weapon to the ready. What had he sensed that I hadn't? "I think I've got an idea. I mean, it's a little crazy but it might just get us across the river."

I didn't want to get my hopes up, but such a smile broke out on Kyle's face. "Tell me."

"What if we used the mud to cover our faces, arms, whatever, any exposed skin that makes us different from the government forces. What if we just strolled across the bridge, two more soldiers heading toward the front?" When I didn't say anything, Kyle continued, "I know it's a little out there, but I don't see how we have many options."

I remained silent. Was this really our only viable option? A madcap idea to walk out into the open, smeared in mud, hoping that it was mistaken for our actual skin tone.

"Well?" asked Kyle, the excitement fading with his smile.

I let out a breath. It really had come to this. Trying to sum up some confidence in the plan, I said, "It might just work. I think we should run with it. The sooner the better, we need as much darkness as possible for this to work." I gripped Kyle's shoulder. "Good plan, my friend."

Kyle beamed at this, then proceeded to kneel forward, thrusting both his hands into the mud pile. I crawled over the jungle floor, until my hands met the thick quagmire. I turned looking for Kyle, but the darkness had cloaked him. I shook my head. Was this really going to work? What option did I have? I pushed my hands in. The stench became overpowering, the rank odour was as bad as the latrine areas of our march. Being exposed to that probably stopped me from throwing up. That, and having a virtually empty stomach. Taking a deep breath, I pushed my face to my hands, smearing the mud all over. I moved down my neck, plunging my hands back a second time, then smearing my arms. When I was satisfied that my camouflage was as good as it would get, I stood. It didn't take long for the smell to diminish as the mud dried to my skin, the pinching sensation a minor irritant.

I returned to Kyle, similarly mud-crusted, only just visible in the minimal light.

"You ready?" he asked.

"I guess so. We've no other option but to go for it. Besides, I didn't just go covering myself in shit for nothing."

I snapped the stock out from my AK and handed it to Kyle who held it in tentative hands. I bent down and retrieved my tac vest, zipping it up. Kyle returned my weapon. "Let's go."

We retraced our steps as best we could, back toward the road, always cautious of being discovered. Our way was clear, and after a forty minute trek with Kyle's arm on my shoulder for safety, we found the road. Kyle's hand fell away. In silence, we followed the edge of the trail, mindful for any sound or sight of human presence. Nothing. We walked until the sound of water rushing by could be heard, past the trees and wall of darkness. Around a bend in the road, a flicker of light filtered through the undergrowth. Without thought, both Kyle and I rushed into cover. In a crouch, we moved forward, my AK stock held to my shoulder. The iridescent light resolved into a small bonfire, off to the right, fifty metres away, the bridge waited. Three armed men stood by the fire, gazing into the dancing flames. They all smoked, huddled together. Swaying slightly, it seemed to me that they weren't smoking a traditional cigarette. This could work in our favour.

Kyle leaned in close, whispering to my ear, "Is there only three of them?"

"I'm not sure, could be more."

Kyle pulled me back, further into cover. "How we going to play this?"

"They're looking into the fire, this works for us. Their night sight will be impaired. I think they're smoking something, one of them didn't seem all that steady on his feet. I say we jog past, if they notice, just raise a hand, wave and continue on. If things go tits-up bolt for the other side of the bridge."

"And if it's guarded on the opposite side?"

I rubbed beneath my nose, sniffing. Mud crumbled from my face. It flaked on parts of my arm, too. It needed to happen now. "Come on." I stood, pulling Kyle up, too. We stepped onto the dirt road. I started to jog, not a panicked sprint, but with enough haste to suggest we knew where we were going. Kyle breathed heavily as we went. None of them turned.

"This is stupid," panted Kyle. "If they look over, we're dead."

"Shut up! Keep going!"

Darkness was still our ally for the moment and we wouldn't be passing close to the fire, not enough for the guards to notice us in any great detail. I hoped. A few feet from the bridge, one of the guards moved. Kyle made a sound like he was having a heart attack, a sharp intake of breath. He kept jogging, his feet thudding on the wooden decking of the bridge. I slowed my jog, raised a hand to the curious guard. His weapon stayed down. Affecting my best Liberian accent, I kept it short, saying, "Need to go."

The guard waved me on, returning to the fire. My heart beat to the point of being painful. It had worked. Kyle must have been across the bridge now, not encountering anyone on the other side. I sped up and followed. Clearing the bridge, I found Kyle bent over, hands on knees.

"It worked," he said between gasps.

"No time." I grabbed his arm and propelled him off the road and back into the bush. We moved deeper into the jungle again.

"Holy fuck, buddy. It really did work."

"I know. I thought we were dead, I really did."

Kyle started laughing, one he attempted to suppress with a hand over his mouth. I didn't blame him, there was always an exhilaration at times like that. I urged him to silence, between a hardly contained laugh of my own.

"Sorry," he said, mastering his laughter.

"Come on, let's go down to the river and wash this shit off."

One barrier crossed. One step closer to Voinjama.

Chapter Fourteen

Kyle's body trembled. I kept one hand over his mouth, pushed his head down into the dirt with the other. Since crossing the bridge we encountered sporadic government soldiers filtering through the jungle. We laid under a tangle of stinging vines, the thorns tearing our clothes and flesh. One snagged my ear. I grimaced, managing to keep from making a noise.

A mismatch of voices drifted toward us. Moments later, the breaking of vines underfoot.

Three times since escaping the gully we'd been forced to hide from government soldiers. We still wore the crimson-stained camo jackets. We needed to be invisible, like ghosts in the forest. Even with the splashes of red, under the thorns we were well hidden.

Six soldiers came crashing through the undergrowth. I pushed myself tighter to the jungle floor. It didn't aid in masking us, but it made me feel better. They were close, only about twenty feet away. Relaxed, their weapons held low, laughing as they moved. I only caught a few words, enough to know they were talking about killing a LURD soldier. It was the last soldier in the line, a painfully slim man, wearing a discoloured white vest, slack on this thin frame, who drew my attention. Instead of a rifle, he carried a rusty bayonet. Hanging on his belt, a severed head swung back and forth with each step, like a macabre Halloween lantern. A thin rope threaded through the ears, secured the gruesome trophy to his belt. The head, eyes missing, twisted and seemed to look right at me before it turned away. In that fraction of a second, I searched the face, wondered if he had been one of the rebels I trained in Zorzor. There were so many faces now. So many memories of those who were dead, I couldn't place him. I pushed my face into the soil like Kyle. I'd seen enough.

Keeping my eyes closed, a stinging doubt came back. We were close to Voinjama, but so were the government forces. I couldn't let my thoughts drift to safety and the luxury of relaxation. All I could think of was where the next enemy would appear. Who I would have to kill. Could I keep Kyle safe?

"Mark, they're gone," said Kyle, interrupting my descent to despair.

I looked around, releasing my grip on Kyle. I hadn't even realised I'd let my hand slip from his mouth. "We better get going."

Kyle had positioned his camera in front of him, steadied it in the dirt, against a small rock. It captured the progress of the government soldiers. I detangled myself from the thorns. The one in my ear blazed as I pulled it free. Touching a finger to the pain, it came back with blood. Another wound to the many I'd collected. I crawled out, ripping a piece of fabric from my trousers. Kyle followed. Grabbing his camera, he stood next to me and reviewed the film.

"Jesus! You see what that guy was carrying?"

I shrugged. "You see a lot of that here."

Kyle shut off his camera. "Yeah, I figured. After I saw them butcher that poor guy in Zorzor."

"That's just Liberia." I felt like a broken record. How many times had I made excuses for the war?

"You've seen more than just what happened in Zorzor?"

"Now's not the time, Kyle. We need to cover ground."

"Come on, buddy. Just a little about what you've seen."

As much as I wanted to tell Kyle to shut up, I figured it would get him to move so I indulged him. Kyle filmed the vine thicket, where we had hidden.

"What you have to understand about Liberia is it has a majority of Christians. But if you scratch a little under the surface, you'll find that tribal religions still linger. I guess you could say it's kind of a hybrid form of Christianity. For bravery, or to inspire his men, a commander will often butcher a prisoner and feed his heart to his men."

"You've seen this?"

I scanned around, making sure we were still alone. "Not the killing, but the feeding to the soldiers. Most of them were high at the time. You hear stories of worse. I heard of one commander stealing a child, cutting through her back, and removing her heart. Apparently that's the proper way to do it."

"Do you believe that?"

"I don't know. You hear a lot of stories about the war. Probably most of it is bullshit. But … Liberia is brutal. I wouldn't put it past either side. Now, stop filming, we're moving out."

Kyle gave me the thumbs up, and switched off his camera. "Thanks for that. Which way?"

I looked about. We needed to move in the direction of the advancing government troops. "That way." I pointed north-west. "Hopefully we can avoid running into any of the government soldiers again."

"I hope so, buddy." Kyle picked a long thorn out of his arm. After inspecting it for a moment, he pinged it away. "The jungle is thinning. We'll run out of cover soon, won't we?"

"Yes. The closer to Voinjama we get, the less jungle we'll have to hide in. We'll be climbing up into the Wologizi hill range."

"And what happens if Voinjama is in the hands of the government when we get there?"

"We need to keep moving." I didn't want to give voice to the possibility we'd gone through so much only to end in failure. Every hour that passed put more government troops ahead of us, making the path to Voinjama treacherous.

Chapter Fifteen

We ghosted through what little cover was available to us. Several times through the day we halted as government forces crossed ahead of us. I decided it would be best to wait for the cover of night before I chanced negotiating the labyrinth of enemy positions. We found a small cluster of foliage, just enough to cover ourselves and hide until the last of the daylight died.

"Get some sleep, Kyle. I'll keep watch."

Kyle inspected what would be his bed for the next few hours. Finding no poisonous companions, he slumped against a tangle of brush. I knelt across from him, hugging the scant cover. Finding us alone for the moment, I followed him down to the ground. My legs and arms throbbed from the strain of our march. I bled from a dozen places, and the predatory insects loved this. A small swarm fussed about me, but I gave up swatting them away, too tired to care. Kyle laid against that tangled brush, his chest heaved like he'd just run a marathon. It surprised me that he managed to keep up. When the mind was willing, the body would follow. He pulled the cap off the canteen and sucked at it like an infant at the teat. He made several loud sucking sounds before he gave up.

"Do you think we'll find somewhere between here and Voinjama where I can fill this sucker up?"

"Not before the town."

"What a surprise."

Kyle threw the canteen. It clunked against the ground. The noise wasn't great, but it made me check to be sure we were still alone.

"So we wait here until night?" Kyle said, before yawning.

I relaxed, let my cramping legs stretch out before me. "Yeah. A few hours rest here, and then we make a break for Voinjama. There's a couple of small villages before there, we'd do best to avoid them. Tomorrow, and it'll all be over."

"Back on our way home."

"Home," I echoed.

Kyle yawned again, his eyes already closed. "Say, buddy. Tell me how you ended up here," he said, voice slow and full of fatigue. "I mean really. Not your company or that bullshit."

I'd been guarded with Kyle up until now. What did I have to lose by telling him? His camera was dark, tucked under his arm. I leaned back, the harshness of the wood sawing at my skin. Closing my eyes, the words came without second thought. "I didn't know what I wanted to do when I was younger, but from an early age I knew I didn't want to be like my mum. Not like you're thinking, she's the most fantastic person you could ever meet. But she had so much wasted potential. She worked forty-plus hours a week in a fish factory. I remember her coming home at night, stinking of fish and so exhausted she could barely eat her meal. It was fucked up," I told him. "I went to University in Edinburgh. Studied geo-political science. I've always been fascinated by the world, how it works, where it's going to go, you know? I graduated, but couldn't find a proper job. I went to an army recruitment drive and ended up joining a short time later. It's strange when I look back now, I don't know why I joined. I got through my basic training, but hated it. I didn't fit in. At university, I had plenty of friends, in the army, I became a bit of a loner. I had to get out. And did. It was such a relief when I was free from them. I worked a few bar jobs. I hated it. Most of the people and the work. I got offered a job in telesales, sitting in a fucking office all day, pissing people off over the phone. I turned it down. Then one night I got talking to this guy at a party. He was ex-RAF and worked for the company. I guess I impressed him. He told me he needed thinkers and fighters for a job. It was all hush-hush. A year later, I'd gone through a training regime. It took what I learned in the army and built on it, you know I can strip this AK with my eyes closed? They improved my use of maps, modern military tactics. Everything I needed for this place. Of course if I'd known I was coming here I might have thought twice about it. I guess you could say I fell into this job. I miss my old friends from before, though. The only thing about this job, it leaves you kinda isolated …"

I opened my eyes to find Kyle sleeping, his cheeks blew out gently as he snored. I snorted a laugh. "Well, Kyle. You missed out on a story just now."

I laid the AK across my legs, wrapping the strap around my wrist a few times. Again, I checked around us. Darkness crept slowly. Another hour and a half and we could move. The government soldiers would be lighting campfires. Those beacons would allow us to skirt around them and slip through their lines. Or that was the plan anyway. Sleep tried to claim me, my head fell forward, but I fought it. I thought about what happened with the machine gunners. At that moment, it felt repulsive to be sitting wearing their bloody jackets. My morals had fallen by the wayside, left in the wake of the need to survive. Killing never crossed my mind, but I had to survive, to keep Kyle safe if nothing else.

Chapter Sixteen

A hand covered my mouth. I opened my eyes, greeted by darkness. Panicked, I reached out, my hands finding a body in front of me. I went for the throat.

"Calm down, buddy. It's me," whispered Kyle. "You were mumbling in your sleep."

I let go of Kyle's neck, relaxing slightly. He didn't move his hand from my mouth. I protested, tapping a finger against his restraining hand. It wasn't tight enough to hurt, but it was uncomfortable.

Still whispering, Kyle said, "I heard something going past not long ago. Couldn't tell what it was."

I nodded and he removed his hand. He didn't move, staying close to me. I remained still, too, my breathing slightly erratic. We listened, but I couldn't detect anything other than the usual murmurs of the jungle. The hooting of some kind of a bird. The rustling of the undergrowth, but nothing to suggest the movement of men.

"I think we can risk moving now," I told him.

Kyle leaned back, letting out a groan. "You could have told me you spoke in your sleep. I just about shit myself when I heard a voice."

"I didn't know. What did I say?"

"Not words as much as noise …"

I looked up at the roof of endless black. "You ready?" I asked.

"I guess so. I'm so tired. I've never felt like this before. In the morning we should reach Voinjama, right?"

"The evening at the latest. It depends if we run into trouble or not."

"Let's pray for no trouble then," he said. "You got a flashlight? I can't see shit."

"I had one, don't really remember what happened to it. Even if we did have one, we couldn't risk it."

"And what if we walk of the side of a cliff."

"It's pretty flat from here to Voinjama."

Blindly, I checked my AK, making sure everything was as it should be. It was. My legs ached, just as my ass did. I struggled to my feet, using the rifle to aid me. My joints seized up, cracking loudly with the motion. I wished for rain, or a freshwater stream, anything to quench my thirst. My throat felt like tiny shards of glass had lacerated it. Thirst was a hard thing to ignore. It didn't disappear with fear, or illness.

"Over here, buddy."

I followed the sound of Kyle's voice, almost stumbling into him. I slung the AK over my neck, threading my arm through the sling. We linked arms, it was the safest way to travel. It would be slow, but steady.

"How the hell did we end up like this, buddy?"

"Best to just think about how we'll get out of it. Come on, we need to cover a few miles in the dark tonight. If I squeeze your arm, it means don't speak. So make sure you don't."

Kyle squeezed my arm. "Sorry. Couldn't resist."

We set off blindly. I held an arm out before me. The trees arrived in my limited vision almost before I could step around them.

Chapter Seventeen

The campfires clearly marked where the government forces holed up for the night. When we first came to a fire, I whispered to Kyle not to look directly into it. The flames robbed the unwise of their night vision. A precious advantage, one we needed to protect. I'd lost count at how many camps we passed. Our progress slowed, the lack of enough light more to blame than the terrain.

A large fire blazed some way off before us. Shadows huddled around it, a joyous chorus of voices lingered in the night. They were happy, perhaps confident of a final victory. And why wouldn't they be? The government was close to delivering the killing blow to the LURD. When the death knell came, it would sound like laughter and gunshots. Sweet scents of roasting meat wafted out to us on the light breeze. Hunger urged us to take the camp, to feast. My mind told us to walk on, yet my legs lagged, each step heavier than the last. Food forgotten, we pushed on.

We moved slowly, crouching as we skirted the fire. No sentries were posted. Confidence in the enemy ranks seemed high. Creeping past was uneventful, if unnerving. My legs ached with the strain of squatting and moving.

There were no more fires in the distance. Had we crossed the front lines of the government troops? Perhaps, but there was no way to know for sure. Kyle obviously thought so, he began to speak again.

"I can see a little better out here. The sky's clearer."

I looked up, the night sky feeling less oppressive. "Yeah, I think you're right." Our path opened before us, revealed in light. I could now pick out obstructions a few feet before we reached them. I let go of Kyle.

"What do you remember of the two soldiers, the ones with that machine gun?" asked Kyle, his voice subdued.

I left the question hanging as I stepped over a fallen trunk. "Everything."

"I remember the feeling that shot up my arm as I hit him on the head. How it sounded. I remember choking back vomit as I tried to end his life. You know how fucked up that is? Were you the same?"

I thought back to it. Everything was a haze of movement, fear, and action. "It needed to be done."

"How can you be so fucking calm? We killed those men. We did."

I stopped and grabbed Kyle's arm. "No, not we. It was me. All me!" I brought my face close to his, feeling the warmth of his breath on my face. "All you did was set up the kill. Does that make you feel better? Does that comfort you a little? I killed them."

Kyle stared at me, his mouth open, sucking in air like he was suffocating. "How do we go back from this, Mark? I don't know how to go back."

Rain fell, a light spray at first, refreshing almost. All too soon it transformed into a deafening deluge. Kyle looked at me, water streaming down his face. I wanted to hit him, punch the fucking panic from him. Did he not want to survive to see home again? It was war. Maybe not our war, but a conflict we were stuck in the middle of. Comforting morals no longer applied. The rules changed. I thought Kyle understood this.

"Do you want to go home?"

"What kind of a question—"

"Do you want to go home?" I asked, anger spilling into my words.

"Of course I do."

We shouted at each other, blinking rain from our eyes.

"Then take this." I pulled the Glock from my leg holster. The weapon was chambered and ready to be fired. I held it out at Kyle, pushing it into his chest. Hard.

He stepped back, his hands up in defence. "I'm not a soldier, Mark."

Again, I pushed into his chest. He grasped the pistol weakly in his hands. "I can't keep you safe unless you help me. You might have to shoot someone. If you don't, we die. You want to live? Then you kill. This is a rule."

Kyle shook his head as if dazed. "No. No, not going to happen. I … I can't. I'm a reporter, not a soldier."

I lashed out, his words moving me to act before I could stop. It wasn't a punch, rather a backhanded slap to his face. It was enough, he fell backwards. The Glock fell from his grasp. I could just make him out in the dark. He stared up at me, his shaking hand soothing his cheek.

"Stop with your bullshit, Kyle. I can't take it. I never know what I'm going to get with you day from fucking day. You drag us down when you're like this. I need your help. Help us get home. Now come on, get up."

I held a hand out. He paused for a moment before grabbing hold. I pulled him up, his weight feeling double to how it did a few days ago.

"Aren't you forgetting something?"

"Guess I am." Kyle rubbed his chin. He searched about the ground with his feet until he found the weapon. He bent and picked it up. I half expected him to hand it back to me. Instead, he tucked it into the waistband of his trousers without comment.

"Don't put it there," I said, turning. "It goes off and you lose your bollocks." It wouldn't happen; the Glock's safety features prevented this. I wanted to piss Kyle off a little. Give him a taste of his petty attitude.

Kyle said something, but I began walking, I thought it best not to speak for a time. I heard Kyle's clumsy presence following me.

The rain continued as we slogged through the night. Kyle tapped my shoulder, I didn't stop but inclined my head.

"Mark, I'm sorry."

"Forget it."

"No, it's not right. I've been selfish. I just don't know how to deal with all this. I'll make this up to you. I don't know how, but I will."

Nothing more was said. We walked until the rain stopped, and the sun rose.

That morning, we came across an abandoned camp. Nothing more than a slight depression in the ground, large enough for three men. A small fire, ringed by stones, reduced to glowing embers. A few pieces of clothing, a t-shirt, and a pair of once white socks, sodden with the rain, lay discarded. On top, some spent shell casings. And one full canteen. A Godsend. Whose camp it was, I couldn't say. It looked to have been abandoned in a hurry. I was just thankful for the little water. We moved off, knowing the owners could return at any moment. One mouthful of water each. That's all I allowed. It wasn't much, but it kept us alive. Kyle drank his mouthful without protest.

I'd got things wrong, misjudged distances. I thought we were only a half-day's march from Voinjama. Two days passed with Kyle and I moving ever northward. Neither of us really spoke, resigned to keep moving. The jungle all but forgotten, we walked over level ground, through long grass swaying about our knees.

Soon we found roads, sandy reminders of civilisation which were missing in the jungle. We rested awhile. I patted Kyle on the back as he sucked in air, hands resting on his knees. He nodded, not able to speak. My throat burned. What I wouldn't have given for an endless supply of water, maybe some painkillers. Grasping Kyle by the arm, I urged him to move again.

"I can't take this anymore," he said, his smile forlorn.

"We can do it. Just keep moving."

Nameless villages popped up, we gave them a wide berth, passing without incident. It was impossible to tell whether they were populated with friendlies. Enough greenery remained as we walked that we could hide ourselves if the need arose. It didn't. No evidence of fighting could be found. No bodies, no gunshots, nothing. It would've been too easy to relax, to let myself believe we were free of the government forces. I acted as if we were still deep within enemy territory. Scanning ahead, checking behind, my AK always grasped in my hands.

Our water supply ran dry. We were both thirsty, and ravenous with hunger. My stomach felt like it was trying to eat itself, a stabbing sensation shot through it with every step. Thoughts of food made the bile rise. It was almost like I'd forgotten how to eat, desperately needing to.

"You think we could slip into that village to get some water? I don't know how much longer I can go on without. Even some rain would help."

The village looked innocent enough, rude buildings clustered round a clearing. They surely had water but what else would there be? A dozen government soldiers, sharpening machetes, eyeing our necks? It wasn't worth the risk.

"Another hour, Kyle. We'll reach Voinjama in an hour."

"I hope so."

I'd developed a cough overnight. Each time I spluttered, my chest and the back of my throat burned. I was miserable. The nagging voice in my head told me to slump to the ground and sleep. At that moment, I didn't really care if I'd wake up or not. Somehow I carried on.

"You know, I think we can ditch these jackets now. Don't want any LURD to shoot before realising who we are," I said.

The rain washed most of the blood out of the fabric. I let it slip from my shoulders. I was happy to be out of a dead man's jacket. Kyle ripped at his as if it were ablaze, throwing it to the ground.

"Fucking thing," he muttered. Kicking it away, he turned his back on it.

In the distance, movement caught my attention. "Down," I said.

Liberia-installed reaction bordering on the superhuman. Kyle and I were down amongst the long grass before the word faded.

He snaked up next to me, eyes following where I pointed.

"You sure you saw something?" he asked, squinting.

"One figure, just for a second."

"We've not seen anyone out here in awhile. There's a lot of villages around. Someone from there?"

The empty campsite we'd liberated the water from bothered me. LURD or government, I didn't know.

"The campsite. Could be someone from there."

"Must be rebels, Mark. We passed the government lines."

I shook my head. "The lines are staggered, fluid, always changing. Overnight, we could have fallen behind the government line without even knowing it."

"So what do we do?"

"We keep going. Not enough water to turn back, or go around. Just stay behind me and keep your eyes open."

Kyle swore again, but didn't say anything further. We both stood. The figure did not appear again which suggested that he hadn't seen us. I braced my AK to my shoulder and moved forward, as quick as my cramping legs would carry me. I kept the weapon trained to where the figure had been, my finger resting on the trigger guard. The effort of keeping the weapon trained made my arms shake.

The acid built up in my muscles. All I wanted was to lower my arms, let go of the heavy weapon. But I couldn't. I needed to focus. The first hint of trouble, I would fire. We couldn't afford the time to wait and question.

We moved past the point where I'd first seen the figure. No sign of him. Beyond lay a small cluster of trees.

"Mark?"

"Keep quiet," I warned. "The trees ahead. They must be there. Come on."

I'd not taken more than a dozen steps when Kyle spoke. "A road. There."

He pointed to the left. A few hundred feet off to our left, a small dirt road cut through the greenery, the red sand gleaming at us.

I'd deal with that in a moment. For now, the trees needed my attention. I moved off again, Kyle tagging along behind me. Voices, not loud. I dashed the last few feet, throwing myself against a tree trunk. Looking around, I almost let out a sigh at the sight that greeted me.

"Tiger King?"

"Tiger King?" echoed Kyle.

I stepped out from beyond the tree into the clearing. Tiger King stood, flanked by one of his soldiers. Two bound men knelt before them, one with a bowed head, the other turned to my arrival.

"It's me, Mark," I said. "Jesus, I thought we were fucked there."

Tiger King gazed at me for a long moment as I walked toward him, his face a mask of neutrality. He waved his machete about the bound men. I'd seen this before, and knew what was coming.

"I thought you dead, Mak. Or run away."

"Where's the rest of your men?" I stood just behind the prisoners. The one who looked up at me seemed to nod, his face covered in dried blood. It took a moment, but I recognised him from Zorzor. Mathew, a name given to him by a missionary. We'd spent a time chatting once, he told me about how he came from the Mandingo tribe. Now he was tied and bound, awaiting execution.

"What's this man done?" I asked, pointing to him. The other prisoner, a young boy wearing a red bandana, I didn't recognise.

"He a coward. Run away from battle."

"What do you mean run from battle? We all ran from fucking battle."

Kyle stepped behind me, a restraining hand on my chest, pulling me away. "No, Mark. Please, let it go. Just let it go."

Everything we'd been through to survive sparked my emotions. Anger. Frustration. We were so close to Voinjama, I didn't want to see more pointless death.

"Watch your tongue, Mak. I cut it out."

With a nod of his head, Tiger King ordered his companion to block me. I still struggled with Kyle. He kept a hand on my AK preventing me from raising it. The soldier approached, standing before us, his mouth open, eyes darting side to side. An AK without a magazine swung wildly about his waist on its strap. He raised his hands, a signal appealing for calm.

I stopped struggling with Kyle. Accepting that Tiger King was about to murder more men, I watched with impotent detachment. It didn't take long, the prisoner with the bowed head died after two strikes, his head cleaved almost in two. Kyle looked away, but I wouldn't. Tiger King stepped before the condemned LURD, Matthew, kicking him in the chest and knocking him back. With two steps, Tiger King loomed over the fallen fighter. He placed a foot on his head, anchoring him in place. The helpless fighter cried out. Tiger King slashed at the exposed neck like he was hacking rope. Slash after slash, the machete reduced his neck to a shredded mess, arterial blood sprayed about the camp.

I watched Tiger King's face as he admired his handiwork. He didn't even try to hide the smile. It should have shocked me, but it didn't. He loved war. Revelled in the killing. Tiger King was at home bathed in blood, and dealing death.

The soldier restraining us looked nothing more than a frightened boy after the carnage.

My body tensed, I'd been shaking all through the execution.

"What are you going to do?" whispered Kyle.

Tiger King wiped his face, smearing blood up to his forehead. He spat a wad of the other man's blood and saliva, and motioned me to approach. I did. I moved halfway toward him, but stopped short.

"Those men didn't have to die so close to Voinjama." My fist clenched around the grip of the rifle. It felt hot in my hands. My head swam with visions of stomping Tiger King's face into the earth. He deserved death.

"I take their skulls. They not follow me. They die. Just like—"

"Engine!" Kyle shouted. "I hear an engine."

The images subsided, the heat dissipating. We all searched for the source. A dirty white pickup raced past on the road parallel to us. Kyle was already on the ground as I pulled the young soldier down with me.

Tiger King roared a challenge, pulling the glinting pistol from his belt. He pointed it at the vehicle, firing once.

"No!" I shouted.

He fired again.

The truck, altered by the shots, turned toward us. A large machine gun mounted on the back, probably a .50 calibre, opened up on us. Tiger King didn't shirk from the fire. He held fast, emptied his magazine into the fast approaching vehicle. The pounding from the gun blared. I slipped my AK to single shot, taking careful aim for the driver, fired some rounds. The windscreen fractured, the next shot shattered the glass. The pickup bounced wildly.

Tiger King reloaded.

I saw the driver, shades and a dirty yellow headscarf hiding what the shades didn't. I fired at him, each shot punched the rife into my shoulder. His head cracked like a melon, a spray of red blasting the interior of the cab.

The pickup slowed to a halt. The machine gunner still fired. Now with a steady platform, his accuracy improved. Tiger King leapt for cover behind a tree. The rounds tore dirt clumps into the earth where he stood moments before.

With the gunner's attention fixed on Tiger King, I'd been ignored. Lucky for me. In my little ditch, I took aim, flicking the switch to auto, and fired. The gunner crouched behind the cab for cover. Tiny sparks flashed off the metal as my shots struck.

Tiger King fired again, and moved, using the distraction my fire caused. He swept in from the side, like an Olympic sprinter. My magazine ran dry. I reached for a new one, the pocket empty. I looked back to Tiger King. The gunner popped his head over the cab. With deft movement, Tiger King planted his foot on the bumper, climbed up the hood, and launched himself at the startled soldier. They disappeared from view. Grunts came from behind the pickup, then silence. I turned to Kyle. He, likewise, watched where the two disappeared. I climbed to my feet, keeping my distance, keenly aware that my weapon was dry. Tiger King reappeared, looking triumphant. He lifted his hand, showing the severed head of the gunner. He held it up by the neck with both hands now, displaying it like a champion raising the trophy. He gave a cry of victory, the last remaining blood spilling down his body.

Kyle swore behind me.

"Come on, we must almost be at Voinjama. We can be there soon," I said, relieved to see the killing ended.

Tiger King stared, eyes wild from the kill. He threw the severed head at me. It glanced off my shoulder, feeling like nothing more than a football hitting me.

"The fuck you doing?"

"This your fault, Mak." Tiger King waved a hand about the quiet clearing. "My men gone 'ecause of you. They run, should have fight."

"It was suicide to stay and fight. You know this … you know this."

"Can we just get to Voinjama?" Kyle found a voice, thin, ready to break, but a voice nonetheless.

"I go to Voinjama." Tiger King thumped a fist against his chest. Breaking into a grin, he spread his arms wide. "I take your skull, Mak. Eat your heart."

Chapter Eighteen

Tiger King stalked toward me with a smile of pure joy, arms outstretched like a vulture advancing on its prey. In one hand, his gleaming pistol. The other, his bloody machete. I took a step back. Behind me, Kyle's panicked gasps.

"Guys, come on," Kyle pleaded. "We're so close. We don't need this bullshit."

Tiger King continued his advance, his eyes never leaving mine. I knew what was coming. He wouldn't be dissuaded. He came for me, for Kyle, for the thrill of killing. I looked down at my rifle, wishing for just one round. I slipped it off its sling, grasping it by the barrel and wielded it like a primitive club. I traced figures of eight in the air, praying for a miracle that would never be answered.

Still, Tiger King advanced like a tsunami enveloping all behind him. I couldn't run. I was close to exhaustion already, where Tiger King looked as though he could run a marathon and still have time for murder.

"Run, Kyle," I urged.

"Where?"

I didn't have the time to answer. Tiger King halted before me. With calm, he slipped his pistol into the waistband of his trousers. Holding his machete up, he turned the blade around, catching the light. He looked from the weapon, then to me, silently communicating that the steel was my fate. He smiled, thrusting the machete into the soft earth. He left it there, standing like a gravestone.

"We fight, like warriors."

"I don't want to do this, dammit."

Tiger King laughed, balled his fists. He looked beyond me. "Kill 'im," he instructed with a nod of his head. I glanced back, just long enough to see the lone soldier spring toward Kyle. He was on his own. I couldn't help him.

Tiger King took a sure step forward. I took a chance, mimicking him. Swinging the rifle with as much force as I could, I aimed for his head. A groan of a battle cry slipped from my lips. Tiger King stepped into the swing, far quicker than I thought possible. He grabbed at my wrists, halting my attack before ripping the weapon from my hands and throwing it aside.

I stumbled back, shocked that I'd been disarmed. Tiger King shook his head at me, disappointed in the calibre of our battle thus far, before pouncing at me with the grace of a starving lion.

I would have run if my legs would have carried me.

I threw a punch at Tiger King's head. He slapped it away, responding with his own swift jab. It rocked my head back, clouding my vision for a moment. I wiped away tears as he came at me again. This time he didn't hold back. He rained blow after blow into my ribs, each one with enough force to break bone. I covered as best I could, my arms pressed hard to my sides. More strikes got through than didn't. I countered when I could, lashing out, but nothing fazed the LURD commander.

He kicked me square in the chest, air bursting from my lungs as I fell back. The ground welcomed me in a harsh embrace. I lay there panting, momentarily forgetting the danger which raced up to me. Tiger King knelt over me. With a knee, and a hand, he pinned my arms over my head. His free hand hammering down into my face, each blow feeling like a brick. I tried to call out to Kyle. What was he doing? Blood flowed into my mouth. I heard the crack of my nose breaking. Another strike. My left eye didn't open again, the near-instant swelling painful. Then, the pressure was gone. My arms flapped uselessly above my face, the feeling slow to return. My face hurt so much I couldn't tell exactly where was injured. Everywhere hurt.

I rolled onto my side, spitting blood into the grass. Stabbing pain grew in intensity with my movement.

Broken rib. I forced out Kyle's name. Twisting until I could see Kyle and the soldier engaged in a clumsy grappling match, Kyle beneath the skinny man, their arms locked together.

A shadow fell across me, blocking out the sun. Tiger King was back, standing over me like a champion gladiator awaiting the sign to complete his victory.

"I 'xpected betta from you, Mak."

He reached down, grabbing me by my tac vest, and pulled me up. My feet dangled in mid-air for a moment. He brought me so close that our noses touched.

His fetid breath washed out as he spoke. "I take you skull, Mak."

I moaned out for Kyle. For anyone. But we were alone. I focused on Tiger King. He savoured my final moments, his smile wide, eyes full of glee.

I wasn't going down without a fight, not after all I'd been through, all I'd done to keep Kyle alive. Tiger King wouldn't take all that away from me.

I let my head fall back, hoping that it seemed I was losing consciousness. The grip holding me in place relaxed. I threw my head forward, slamming the bridge of Tiger King's nose. The head butt hurt me, but hurt him more. He grunted at the impact. I brought a knee deep into his solid stomach, heard him gasp with the shock of it. He dipped forward, allowing me to bring an elbow down on the back of his neck. Tiger King crumpled to the grass. I looked back, Kyle now on top of the soldier, a hand pushing into his face. I took a step toward him, but hearing Tiger King grunt again, realised I needed to finish this.

The machete embedded in the ground waited only five feet away. My steps were clumsy, the weakness in my legs hindering me. Before I could grasp the weapon, a hand grabbed my tac vest from behind, pulling me back.

Tiger King spun me around. With swift movements, he enveloped me in a monstrous bear hug, pulling me into his body. I knew Tiger King was strong, but now I was feeling the full force of his strength. My arms were trapped between our two bodies. Breathing became difficult, almost impossible. A single gunshot rang out. Kyle? I couldn't move to see.

"You die, Mak." He let out a roar, applying more pressure.

The edges of my vision darkened. Each breath came faster than the last. My body convulsed. Searing pain raked through me. My mind dulled, but my finger, held down by our waists, touched something cold. I managed to free my hand for just a moment. Tiger King's pistol sat in his waistband. With every strangled breath I managed to take, I pushed my hand down, penetrating between our bodies. I felt with my index finger until I touched the trigger guard.

"You die, Mak!"

"Fuck you!" I spat out.

I slid my finger over the trigger and pulled it up. The weapon fired down. The pressure disappeared. Tiger King howled. I fell back, struggling for breath, coughing and gulping air. Tiger King lay on the ground, clutching his groin. A dark stain of crimson seeped down into his trousers and onto the grass. He made mewing noises, his teeth clenched and bared.

I struggled to my feet, taking a hesitant step toward Tiger King. I fell again, hard onto my knees. I crawled the last distance to the wounded commander. He kept one hand over his crotch, stemming the blood. The other reached for the pistol. I stumbled, falling onto him. Tiger King pulled the pistol free. I grabbed at his wrist. He was weaker now, much weaker. I wrestled the weapon from his grasp, the blood coating his hand made the gun slip from his lax grip. I slapped it away, watched it fall amongst the foliage. I rolled off him, pulling myself a few feet away. We both lay there in the clearing. The only sounds were Tiger King's pained whimpers, my heavy breathing, and the scuffles between Kyle and the soldier.

I pulled myself upright, groaning with effort, and looked at the wounded warrior. He stared back, his eyes large and unblinking.

"It seems … as though … the tide has turned, motherfucker," I said, stealing breaths. I pulled the machete free from the ground, and returned to standing next to Tiger King. "You know what this is?" I asked, holding the machete out before him. His eyes followed the movement of the blade. "This is payback. Payback for everything you've done out here. Everything you've made me see. Everything you've made me do. And everything you've done to me."

I raised the weapon to strike, but a voice stayed my hand.

"Mark, no!" Kyle stood to my right, his arm out stretched. He shook his head. "You don't need to do this. It's over."

I looked down at Tiger King. More than anyone, he deserved death. Images of the boy he'd beaten at Zorzor filled my mind, the memories fresh and raw. I aimed the machete down to his throat. He didn't beg for his life, only watched in muted fascination.

Kyle's hand rested lightly on my shoulder. "He's not getting up from that wound. Leave him. Let's go home."

I let the steel touch Tiger King's throat. "What happened with the other guy, Kyle?"

"We struggled … and the gun went off. He's dead."

"He dies, too," I hissed.

"You don't want to end up like him."

And something about those words struck me. Tiger King would surely die from his wound. It looked to be arterial bleeding. I'd seen enough killing, enough death. The strength which kept me upright, fled. I dropped the blade, as if it suddenly became hot, repulsed at my previous thoughts.

"We can go home now, Mark."

I didn't say anything. The pain, which for a moment had been eclipsed by my final reserves of adrenalin, returned. I allowed Kyle to support me, slipping my arm over his shoulder, and ignoring the spatter of warm blood on his shirt. Tiger King briefly convulsed before going limp. He'd not wake. It was strange to see him lying unconscious and bleeding to death. So much power he wielded in life, and now, he was just one of the countless corpses that littered Liberia. I realised there was a faint smile on my face. Kyle took a snapshot of him. I didn't ask why, he didn't volunteer the reason.

In silence, we set off for Voinjama.

Chapter Nineteen

The journey to Voinjama was a haze of stumbling, swearing, and Kyle's stuttering encouragement. He kept me going, lending what little strength he had. The terrain crept upward becoming hilly. It felt like Liberia didn't want to let me go, the terrain conspiring to roll me back into the jungle.

"Is that it? Voinjama?" Kyle asked as we glimpsed the city on the cusp of the horizon. It seemed like a jigsaw of mismatched buildings, mixed with trees, nestled in the hills.

I struggled to lift my head, wiping away tears from my good eye. "That's it." It seemed a lifetime ago that I passed through Voinjama on my way to Zorzor. "Give me a second to rest here, Kyle."

"I don't want to wait here for much longer, Mark. God knows those government guys could be right behind us." He glanced over his shoulder.

"I think we're alright here."

"I'm not taking that chance, buddy. Come on." Kyle pulled me onward. "We can rest in the city."

We carried on. Drawing closer we saw figures milling about on the outskirts, like a hive of ants. Soldiers or civilians, I couldn't tell.

"What do we do when they notice us?" asked Kyle. We were close enough to see LURD soldiers preparing defensive positions around the city. Digging shallow trenches, creating roadblocks from the city's debris.

"Get your hands up. Best to do it now."

Kyle let go of me, throwing his hands above his head. I nearly fell with the sudden loss of support. It took every effort to not drop to the ground. I kept my left hand over my damaged ribs. The right, I raised for a moment but the pain was too great. I dropped my hand, placing it on Kyle's shoulder, positioning myself just behind him.

"They've noticed us."

Two armed sentries pointed at us, shouting to their superiors.

"LURD," I called. "Friendly." My weak voice almost certainly wasn't heard.

"LURD," Kyle yelled, taking up my call. A group of LURD rushed toward us, bristling with AKs. They spread out, approaching warily. When they noticed the colour of our skin, a murmur of excitement grew. A few weapons lowered, but most remained trained on us.

"What happens now?" whispered Kyle.

"Wait for the commander."

We all stared at each other over the few metres between us. Some of the LURD relaxed and began smoking, talked amongst themselves. The older members still viewed us with caution, keeping their AKs at the ready, aimed at us.

"I think you can lower your hands for now, Kyle. Make it slow. No sudden movements."

He did as I said, taking hold of me once again. I was thankful, unsure of how much longer I could have stood on my own. A couple of the LURD watched Kyle's action, but generally, we were ignored.

A commotion behind the LURD caused some of the soldiers at the back to turn. A figure pushed through the group to muttered annoyance.

"Mark? Is that you? What the hell happened?"

Joseph Coleman, the team leader from our company, stood amongst the LURD. He waved them away, and rushed to my side. The LURD leisurely returned to their tasks.

"Who are you?" he asked Kyle.

Before Kyle spoke, I said, "He's a friend. I'll explain later."

"Come on, let's get you to somewhere comfortable. You look like shit."

Joseph took hold of me, his strong arms holding me up. Between him and Kyle, they carried me into Voinjama.

"Expecting trouble, Joe?" I asked as we passed the first line of defences.

"The government forces are about ten miles out. If something doesn't change in the next few days, this little rebellion we're propping up will be crushed."

I lapsed into silence. My legs dragged behind me. I'd given up trying to help them carry me. They hefted me up some rickety wooden stairs that creaked under the weight. My eyes closed. More stairs. They laid me on something soft. A mattress, I guessed. It felt perfect, as soft as a cloud. Kyle introduced himself to Joseph. They spoke, but I couldn't follow. I drifted off to sleep. An almost forgotten sleep for me. I felt safe.

Chapter Twenty

"Mark." A hand rocked me gently. "You need to wake up."

I opened my good eye, returning to a world of pain. Before, adrenalin blocked the aches and now I felt its full ferocity. Joe sat on the edge of the bed, looking down at me. Kyle slept in a bunk across the small room.

"How long was I sleeping?" It hurt to speak, my voice little more than a raw whisper.

"Five hours, mate. We patched you up as best we could. You've a broken rib, your nose is broken. I snapped that back in place. You were awake at the time, but not coherent."

Joe handed me a canteen. He cradled my head forward to let me drink. The water slipped down my tender throat, like a flood of little blades. I coughed, spluttering some down myself.

"That's enough for now, Mark." Joe screwed the lid back on the canteen.

"Painkillers?" I rasped.

"You've had them. You'll get more in the next few hours".

Joe ran a hand over his shaved head. He looked at me like a man comforting his son. Whenever something went wrong in the company, Joe blamed himself. They were his men, and I was one of them.

"I knew it was a bad idea to send you forward. It's my fault this happened to you. I'm sorry, Mark. It was a shit call I made."

"I wanted to go. It's not your fault. You know I'd have went even if you said no. They needed someone out there." I motioned over to Kyle. "He tell you the story?"

"Some of it. He was exhausted, slurring his words. I thought I'd just wait for you to tell me. But, Mark, the government forces are only two or three days away. We don't think the LURD will be able to mount a convincing counterattack. We're pulling back into Guiana tomorrow. Our mission is over. You'll be in hospital soon, three or four days at most. Some of the lads might pop in to see you. They've been anxious since you stopped checking in. Satellite phone?"

"Stolen."

Joe nodded and stood. The bed creaked. "I left you a present for later." He pointed to the table. Four dark bottles of beer sat in a cardboard crate. "For the wounds, you know? Medicinal." He reached down, touching my shoulder. "I'll check in with you later. Get some more rest."

He turned to leave and my eyes closed as the door closed behind him.

Chapter Twenty-One

A sharp crack woke Kyle and I. He sat bolt upright, rubbing his eyes. A lone bulb pumped out a murky yellow light in the corner of the room. I took longer, struggling to angle myself against the wall behind the bed.

"What was that?" Kyle swung his legs from his own bed. He crossed to the dirty window, wiped it with his hand, and looked out. The night closed in around our window, obscuring all, only offering a reflected glimpse of our room.

"Gunfire," I said. "It's probably been going on for a while. You know what the LURD are like."

"How can you be sure?"

I shrugged, a movement that caused pain to stab up from my ribs, into my shoulder, and neck. I moaned a curse. "Can't be sure. But if it was anything serious, Joe would come and get us."

Kyle stayed at the window for a little longer, before moving to sit on his bed. "I guess you're right, buddy. Guess I'm just a little jumpy after all that shit." He glanced to the beers. A half smile appeared. "Shall we?"

The painkillers hadn't banished the pain, so why not add some alcoholic medication on top of them? "I think that's a great idea. Pass me one, will you?"

Kyle stretched over, snatching two of the dark bottles. He unscrewed one, handed it over to me, then did the same for his bottle. He reached out, offering his beer in a toast. "What will we drink to?"

"Going home."

Kyle nodded twice, looking down. "Perfect."

We touched bottles and drank. The beer was warm, smelled bad, and had a nasty aftertaste, but I didn't care. The African beer would give me something I needed. A chance to escape from the pain. We drank in silence. I couldn't think of anything to say to Kyle. Most of our conversation previously had pertained to surviving, to escaping to where we were now.

"Joe seems a good guy," said Kyle, rolling the bottle in his hand.

"Yeah, he is. He's the one that got me the job with the company. I owe him a lot."

"He seemed pretty cut up with what went on."

"Shit happens."

I finished the first beer faster than I'd ever before. Kyle dutifully handed me another. I already felt the effects. The pain had dulled, but when I moved my head, the room lurched in a blurry tilt. Painkillers, and the ordeal we'd been through broke down my resilience to alcohol. I drank anyway, unscrewing the cap myself. With each mouthful, I felt myself succumbing just a little more. Kyle finished his first beer, and reached for the last bottle.

"Tastes like shit, huh, buddy?" He flicked the cap across the room. We both watched it spin on its axis before coming to rest.

"Better than nothing." I lay back into the welcoming mattress, stared up at the damp ceiling. It had been white once, but now looked like mouldy cheese. I laughed at it, a roof of cheese.

"What's so funny?" asked Kyle, the smile returning to his face.

"Nothing. Just getting drunk."

Kyle nodded his understanding. More silence followed. I rested the bottle on my chest, securing it with one hand. Thoughts drifted back to Zorzor. They were unwelcome. Tonight would be my escape from them all. It was a relief when Kyle spoke again.

"Why did you come to Liberia, Mark?"

I stared at the cheese roof while I answered. "I told you, the company got the contract and deployed us out here. Some financial backer of the LURD felt they needed military advisors. So that's what we were. Not that it's been that successful, by the looks of things." I pulled a hand down my face. My nose ached, but not as severe as it had been. It was dull, like a memory of an injury. My eye, still swollen shut, felt like it protruded from my socket.

"You know, I was thinking, buddy. I don't suppose you being here is all that legal. I mean, what's the government's position with you here? Don't suppose they like mercenaries … sorry, advisors running around here unchecked."

"Okay, Kyle. First," I said, raising a finger, "Liberia is a backwater. You know yourself, it's hardly mentioned in the media. Everyone is focused on Afghanistan, and what's going on there. Hell, they're even rumours of Iraq next. Second, I'll tell you what the government thinks. They're not blind, they know we're out here, but what you've got to understand is we're filling a role. The government would rather Taylor was ousted. They can't afford to get involved, but if they let a few well organised advisors train the rebels, and in the end get rid of Taylor, so much the better. They can deny involvement, and the world loses a tyrant in the process."

I had some more beer. My head started to spin.

"I see, Mark. I guess I never really thought about it like that before." He laid his bottle on the floor. "You didn't answer my question. Why are *you* out here? Personally?"

The question hung in the air for a while. I finished my beer, letting the bottle roll off my chest, onto the bed. Squeezing my forehead with thumb and index finger, I told him, "What do you think of when you think of back home?"

"What do you mean?"

"Come on, Kyle, it's a simple question. What do you think of?"

Kyle stuttered over a reply, none of which I listened to.

"I'll tell you what I think of. Grey. Rain. Depression. It's all bullshit. The people back there, I'm sick of them. Sick of their lives. All they do is moan, wanting more money. They'd shit on each other, just to climb a little higher, you know what I mean? I mean some of the girls I know, all they care about is fucking handbags, heels, make-up, and looking good. And the guys, all they look for is someone to fuck. Or football. Y'know, shit like that."

I knew I was babbling, and not quite making sense. I should have shut up then, but I didn't.

"I guess I just want more. I thought I'd find it in the army, but I didn't. Out here, with the guys from the company, everything makes sense. You look out for the guy next to you. You become close, you know? I have friends back home, but they don't understand me, not deep down. The guys in the company, that's different. I might not have a single thing in common with them, but I know, without a shadow of a fucking doubt, that I can trust them. You know what I mean?"

Kyle stroked his chin. He took a long pull on his beer. "You don't enjoy anything about being home?"

"Yeah, I've some friends, and family. I can't explain it. Out here, despite all the shit, it makes sense in a fucked up way."

"And the killing."

More silence. I smoothed back my hair. It was greasy and full of dried blood. "I never thought it would come to this. It's funny, I look back to when we first met, I thought I could walk into someone's war and walk out the same way. I mean, who the fuck comes to a warzone and expects that? You know I killed those people for us, so we could survive. You kill if you want to live. It's simple, it makes sense … but I don't like it. I feel sick to my stomach when I think back."

"So you understand why I stopped you with Tiger King?"

I kept quiet, remembering how much I wanted to push the machete blade into his throat. How much I wanted him to suffer an agonising death. And I felt ashamed.

"I couldn't let you butcher Tiger King. He was dying, that was enough. You didn't need to go further."

Tears welled. "He deserved to die," I managed to say, emotion choking me.

"Yes, he did. He needed to die. That's the difference. What you did, that was necessary. What you could have done … well, that would have been too much."

I nodded, wiping at the tears, not wanting to let Kyle see me at my weakest.

"I'm sorry I ran away. I didn't know what to do. I didn't even think I had the Glock until we were on our way to Voinjama. I'm so sorry."

I took a moment gathering myself before speaking, "Don't be, Kyle. If it had been me, I'd have probably done the same. You didn't come here to fight. I'd have done the same."

It was then, even drunk, I noticed that Kyle was crying openly. His words came out on a flood of emotion. "I'll make this up to you. I don't know how, Mark. I don't know when. But I will. You saved me, kept me alive out there. How can I ever repay you?"

I mastered my tears, turned to Kyle, and said, "You don't need to. That last stretch to Voinjama, I wouldn't have made it without you. There's no debt."

Kyle pinged his bottle twice. "Thank you."

I smiled. "It's over now. Tomorrow we'll be travelling through Guiana. The day after, flying back to France."

Kyle leaned back, resting against the wall. "It all feels like a terrible nightmare, one that'll probably stay with me for the rest of my days."

If Kyle's memories were to be a constant nightmare, mine would be a permanent hell. But a hell that would be faced tomorrow. The beer and painkillers saw to that.

"You got enough footage to make your film?"

Kyle shrugged. "I won't know until I see the footage. I've got to take into account spoilage of the data. I'll have enough. I just don't know how I'll report it all."

"It looks like we both have our challenges to face," I said, stifling a yawn. I pyramided my fingers over my chest. "But not tonight. We'd better get some sleep. Joe will want to leave early tomorrow."

"Tell me we've got transport."

"We came in with two flatbed trucks," I said, sleep reaching for me. "We should still have them."

"Music to my ears, buddy. Until tomorrow then."

"Until tomorrow. Get the light, Kyle."

He picked up his empty beer bottle, and threw it at the lone light. It connected, shattering the bulb, destroying itself in the process. The room was plunged into instant darkness. We both laughed.

Outside, someone fired off a few rounds, breaking the calm. Between them, I could hear goats upset by the gunfire. It was a pleasant enough night. The gunfire, sparse enough to not cause me concern. It had become a faithful companion accompanying my sleep.

Kyle yawned. "Only the dead have seen the end of war."

"What's that?" I asked, barely awake.

"Something you said to me when we first met. You remember?"

"Not really."

Silence.

"Do you think you've seen the end of war, Mark?"

I thought about that question. Kyle's breathing became softer, filled with small grunts, sleeping.

Had I seen the end of war? "No, I don't think I have."

I wasn't dead.

Chapter Twenty-Two

The thumping in my head rattled my brain as much as the banging on the door. Kyle leaped from his bed, fists clenched.

"It's alright," I said. "Door."

Kyle swore, wiping his face with his dirty shirt. "I was back in the jungle there. I just about shit myself," he said, puffing.

When he pulled the door open, only the slightest of light shone through the slivered gap. I couldn't make out who was there.

"You the reporter?" someone said.

"Ah, yeah," answered Kyle.

"We're bugging out in five minutes. Get your shit together."

Kyle looked around the room, then down at himself. I did the same. We were both wearing our shit. It's all we managed to take back from Zorzor.

I craned my neck, peering through the dimness. "Andrew? That you?"

"Sure is. I came to see you last night, but you were out of it, mate. We'll talk later. Joe wants us to get out asap. Seeing us packing up is making the LURD nervous."

I nodded in agreement. "We'll be down in a minute."

"See you out there." Andrew's shadow paused for a moment. "It's good you got out, Mark. Welcome back," he then said, turning to leave.

"I can hardly believe we're going to make it out of here, buddy," said Kyle, closing the door. He slipped on his vest, carrying the precious SD cards, the documented evidence of our time together.

I drained the last of the canteen Joe left the night before. My throat still burned, but less so since the painkillers. Taking three deep breaths, I struggled to sit up in the bed. The broken rib thrust into my side, making me suck in air. Kyle rushed to my side, helping me to sit up, then stand. I swayed a little, my head not completely clear of the night before.

"Thanks, Kyle. Listen. I think I might have spoken a load of shit last night. My head wasn't in the best place. And the beer and painkillers didn't help much. Whatever I did say, I wouldn't take too much notice of."

My conversation with Kyle the night before was now just words and feelings. I couldn't remember what I'd said, just that it was probably something best kept to myself.

"You didn't say anything wrong. Don't worry about it." Kyle gave me a smile, one that crept from the side of his mouth. I didn't entirely believe him.

"Help me get down the stairs, will you?"

Kyle nodded, opening the door, and supporting me as I shuffled out. The floorboards creaked with each step. The stairs seemed smaller than normal. Each step down, took longer than it should. Kyle didn't complain, matching me step for step, offering words of caution when I swayed forward a little.

We emerged from the two story shack, into the dim morning. A haze of moisture blew in on the slight breeze. It was refreshing since being cooped up in the tiny, sweltering room. Our truck waited a little up the street. The men from the company busied themselves loading it with equipment, and bags. Joe gave us a wave as we lumbered toward him. He swung his AK to his back, and jogged over to us.

"Glad you didn't sleep in," he said smiling. "I'll take over here. Thanks, Kyle."

They passed me between them, Joe taking the burden from Kyle. We walked on a little before Joe said, "Kyle, I've pulled some strings," said Joe. "We can get you on our plane, but once back in France, you're on your own. Can you get back to the States from there?"

"Sure I can. And thank you. I didn't know what to do. The thought of being stuck here just …"

"We wouldn't leave you," I said. "Not after what we've been through. Or what's about to happen."

"Which is why we need to leave now."

Joe guided me to the truck. He hefted me up into it with a grunt. Strong hands took hold from the back, pulling me over. I hissed, my ribs aching from the movement. Kyle climbed in after me, then Joe. He slapped the hood of the cab twice, and sat down next to me. The rest of the guys from the company greeted me with friendly comments. I smiled, answered a few, but couldn't take the conversation further. My eyes closed, there was nothing I could do to resist. I felt the movement of the truck as it negotiated the ill-kept, pothole-scarred road. I heard voices around me, but it all faded into the background as sleep took me once again.

Chapter Twenty-Three

"Where am I?"

"At Conakry airport, buddy."

I opened my good eye, thick with a crust of rheum. I touched a tentative finger to my closed eye. It ached, but more dull than anything. The swelling felt as if it had gone down some.

"We can't be. We were just on the truck."

"Two days ago. Joe thinks he gave you too many painkillers. He wasn't sure of the dosage. Knocked you out clean."

I struggled to rationalise the situation. Kyle sat in a chair by the window. An air-conditioning fan buzzed overhead, the blades rhythmically chopping away. There wasn't the overpowering smell of damp, or rot. Was Liberia behind us? The bed, far from luxurious, was adequate. There was even a box television set resting on the desk, next to me. We'd really left the depredations of war behind.

"The plane's due in an hour or so. Everyone's grabbing some sleep while they can."

"Not you?"

"Only one bed, buddy. I didn't fancy spooning with you. You don't smell that fresh, you know?"

As I looked closer at Kyle, it was clear he'd showered and shaved. The patchy stubble which marred his features was gone. His hair, clean, fluffy almost. He now wore a pair of Hawaiian shorts, a plain white shirt, and a pair of sandals. One dangling off his foot as he tapped it on the floor.

"Running water, huh?"

"Feel like a new man," he said, waving a hand down his face and body. "If you need me to, I can help you get in the shower, just ask. Promise I won't peek."

"Yeah, maybe later." Kyle had seen it all before. I'm sure neither he nor I really wanted to see it again.

"Might help with that itching," his voice dropped to a conniving whisper, "down below."

"Yeah. Later." The pain in my face and side far eclipsed the itchiness of down there. I laughed. It was good to laugh. Kyle held something, cupped in his hands. "What's that?"

"The SD cards. Looks like they all survived. It's just … I don't know if I can watch the footage, or look at the pictures." He jingled the fragile data cards like loose change. "I know it must sound retarded since it's what I came to see. It just all feels so personal. Does that make sense?"

"Yeah, it does." I paused, considering my words. "You came to Liberia to document the war, the people here. You didn't expect you'd become involved in the story. It's one thing to look through a lens and speak. It's another to be part of it. It's almost like it's your story now."

"Jeeze, Tiger King must've knocked some sense into you. Ah, shit." Kyle fell to silence for a moment, his face twisting into a pained expression. "Sorry about that, I wasn't thinking."

"It doesn't matter." I waved away his apology. "What I was saying, it's now yours. It'll make it easier to tell. It's always easier telling your own story than someone else's."

"Speaking from experience?" asked Kyle, eyebrow raised.

"Speaking shit probably."

We both laughed. I shifted to get more comfortable, my arm above my head. Perhaps it was because Kyle washed, but the stench from my armpits caught my throat, almost making me gag.

I struggled to swing my legs out of the bed, and stood. "I can't think of anything I'd rather be right now other than clean."

"Sorry to say, Mark but you stink. You need some help getting to the shower?"

I waved Kyle away, shaking my head. "I think I'll manage. You couldn't try and find something for me to wear, could you? I lost all my spare clothes on the trail."

"Sure," said Kyle patting down his shirt. Can't promise you'll look as stylish as I do, though."

He left, laughing at his own joke. I ambled over to the bathroom, using the doorframe for support. Kyle left the room in such a mess it was like a bomb had gone off. His filthy clothes lay scattered on the floor, mixed with the used towels. He'd left me only one small towel, but I didn't care. I just wanted to be clean, to wash the final remnants of Liberia off me. I peeled my t-shirt off and over my head, wincing at the rib that stabbed my side. I then stepped out of my trousers and finally my boxers. For a moment, I stood enjoying the new sensation of being naked, knowing a warm shower was to follow. The little ventilation grill over the door rattled, bringing me back. I took one of Kyle's soaked towels, and wiped down the large mirror behind the sink. I was anxious to see the legacy of Liberia. I cleared enough to be able to see myself. I couldn't help the hand that rushed to my face. Looking back at me was someone I didn't know. I'd lost so much weight, lost some muscle tone. Around my ribs, on both sides, dark bruises marred my skin from where Tiger King attacked. But there was a change beneath the skin. One I didn't want to recognise.

My eye, swollen shut, took on a dark-purple colouration. I touched it again, it didn't hurt as much as it had before. There was a pressure building in it. I should have been more worried, but that was something for the doctors to concern themselves with. I didn't look down, the itching telling me all I needed to know.

I reached into the tiny box shower, switched it on. A weak stream fell from the showerhead. I put a hand under the water. It was just the right temperature, cold by British standards, I guess, but perfect for West Africa. I stepped in, a sigh escaping my lips, my arms spread to either side of the cubicle for support. It was another world, one that I'd taken a nightmarish holiday from. It was refreshing to be back. The water went over my head, washing the muck from my hair. It disappeared down the drain as I began to scrub at my body with an inadequate bar of yellow soap.

I stayed in the shower until I heard Kyle return. Reluctant as I was to come out, I knew time was precious. France, Guiana's former colonial masters, were the only European nation to operate flights in and out. These were rare, to miss one would mean being stranded for a few days longer than needed. I wrapped the small towel around my waist, barely covering myself, and stepped back into the bedroom.

"Feel better?" asked Kyle handing me a rough bundle of fabric. "That's all Joe had. Sorry, buddy."

I inspected the tangle of clothes, unravelling it. "Yes, much better. You wouldn't believe the filth that came off me." I pulled out a pair of joggers, and a grey t-shirt. They looked about the right size. "These are fine," I said, throwing the remaining pile onto the bed.

"How's your ... ah, rash?" asked Kyle, as I went back to the bathroom to change.

"The same," I called back. "You don't want to see it."

"That's right, I don't."

Freshly changed, I came back to the bedroom, laughing. We were both a little giddy with the prospect of getting out of Africa.

"You're moving a little better."

"Yeah, the shower loosened my muscles up a bit." I perched on the edge of the bed. Kyle scribbled into a small notepad. "What are you doing there?"

"This," he said, stabbing the pencil onto the paper, "is a list of my contact details. Address, phone number, email. I'd like to keep in contact with you … y'know, after now. When things are back to normal."

I hadn't thought about after Liberia, or keeping in touch with Kyle. I suppose after all we'd been through it was a natural desire. He ripped off the page, handing it to me. I nodded my thanks, folded it, and placed it into my pocket. In the short time Kyle and I were together, we'd forged a friendship closer than one that would have been possible in the real world. It would have been strange to say goodbye to Kyle at this point, and not see him again.

"Here," he said, handing me the notepad. "Give me yours."

I scribbled down my information. Kyle took back the notepad, briefly looking at what I'd written down. He flipped it closed and slipped it into his pocket.

"We should go," he said. "Don't want to miss that flight. Oh, that reminds me." He pulled at the waist of his shorts, sticking his hand down. He pulled out a passport, sealed in a clear plastic bag and covered with specks of dirt. "Didn't want to chance losing this." He patted his crotch. "Safest place for it."

"I guess so," I said. Joe held my passport, and travel papers. Guinea was a nation that didn't tolerate foreign nationals running around. The company paid the appropriate bribes to the right people to allow us access. Kyle on the other hand, how had he gotten in?

"What about your travel papers, Kyle?" I asked, interested in his own arrangements to get into this secretive nation.

"Ah!" He opened the bag, removing his passport. Inside, folded several times like a treasure map, was a single sheet of paper. He took care opening the folds. I caught a glimpse of the Republic of Guinea seal. He held it up for me to see. I squinted, my impaired vision less than it should have been.

"That looks official."

"It is," he said proudly. "It should be, too. Cost enough. I blew most of my budget just getting to Liberia."

"Hope it was worth it, my friend." I almost stuttered over the last word. After all we'd been through, that's what Kyle was now, a friend. He'd kept me going at the end. Perhaps he'd even given me the drive to keep going when, if alone, I'd have surrendered to exhaustion and despair.

"Time will tell, buddy. Shall we? I've had enough of Africa."

I nodded, and without asking he was by my side taking my arm, helping me walk from the room. Outside our temporary lodgings the humidity was stifling. It was hard not to miss the air-conditioning the room possessed. We walked to Conakry airport's international terminal. Joe and the others were waiting, surrounded by baggage. Dotted around the airport were Guinean Gendarmeries, and soldiers, their red berets marking them out. None looked friendly, all stood watching us, faces like stone. Some appeared a little too young, all dangerous. Either we were a rare sight, or unwelcome. Probably both. Anyone else should have been intimidated, but nothing fazed me anymore, and not when we were going home.

Joe went about handing us our papers and passports. He stopped at Kyle and I, exchanging a few words, asking how we were. Patting me on the back of the neck, he left to continue handing the rest out.

I opened mine, flipping through until I found my picture. I held it up next to my face and turned to Kyle. "See the resemblance?"

Kyle let out a low whistle. "Jeeze, I don't think your own mum would recognise you." He looked between my face and the picture. "You sure they're going to let you out looking like that?"

"We'll see," I said. "Look." I pointed out the window of the terminal to the runway. A small, propeller-powered Air France flight taxied into position.

Kyle patted me on the back. "Will you be alright? I should go and make sure they let me through the gate."

"I'll be fine. You go get yourself checked in."

"I'll see you on the plane, buddy."

"Sure you will," I said, giving him a soft push. "Get going."

I watched Kyle head to the gate. I hobbled over to the row of seats where the company guys sat in excited conversation, and plopped myself down in an empty seat. This was it. I was finally going home.

Chapter Twenty-Four

Charles De Gaulle airport was alive with a swarming of humanity and yet no one paused to look at us, an odd assortment of men waiting on baggage. I watched the endless procession of bags trundle around on the conveyor belt. Joe stood to my right, near enough to catch me if I faltered, but far enough to give an illusion of independence.

He leaned in. "You alright?"

A small boy, clutching his mother's hand peered at me. When I stared back, he stepped behind her legs with inquisitive eyes. Couldn't really blame him for watching me. I must have looked a fright to the kid. It struck me that in Liberia, a few more years and he would have probably already fired his first weapon.

"Mark?"

"I'm fine, Joe," I said, tearing my eyes away. "Just wish the bag would hurry up."

"If you want to grab a seat, I'll get them. We've got a minibus to take us to hospital."

"I'm better standing right now."

Joe didn't look convinced, his brow furrowing.

"I'll be fine," I repeated.

He nodded, and turned to speak to the group. If I sat, I would have fallen asleep. I didn't want to sleep, not until I was in a bed. Besides, I hadn't said goodbye to Kyle. I hadn't seen him on the plane, sleeping most of the way to Paris. He disappeared once we landed, off to make some calls to get himself back to the States probably.

A blaring announcement went out over the speakers. A few people hurried off. I picked out the familiar form of Kyle weaving through the congregated throng, carrying a steaming plastic cup. I wished, in that moment, that I had a picture of him from when we first met. He looked so different, only I couldn't pinpoint what had changed. In that first meeting I never dreamed that my survival would have one day depended so much on him.

"You've no idea how much I've missed coffee," he said, tipping the cup toward me. "You want some?"

I shook my head. "No, you're right. You all set for heading home?"

Kyle blew on his drink. "Yeah, think so. Got a flight out tomorrow. Dublin, then on to New York. Think I'll be sleeping in one of those chairs tonight. Don't have the money for a hotel and the flights. Sucks, but you won't hear me complain. What about you?"

"Once the bags come through we're all off to hospital. It's routine, we get checked out, then head home."

"I'm sure it'll be a few days at most you'll be kept in. You're tough, buddy."

It didn't matter to me. I could have spent months in hospital and I wouldn't have uttered a word of protest. It was safe there.

"You know I was thinking something as I walked back here," Kyle said.

"What's that?"

"All these people …" He motioned with his cup at those around the airport. "They've not seen or experienced half of what we have. The things we've seen, the things we've done and survived. How many people can say they've done that? It's something special."

"Special, just not in a good way."

Kyle chewed his lip. "You're right. I don't know what I'm trying to say. It's just that I don't feel like the same person I was when I went into Liberia. How about you?"

Numb. It was the only word to describe how I felt. "I'm too sore to think right now. I don't know what to feel about everything."

"Doesn't matter, I suppose. We made it out." Kyle shrugged and took a sip of his drink. "I gotta tell you, buddy, when I stepped foot in Africa, I didn't think it would be like this. I thought I would snap a few pics, do some interviewing, film a little shooting, then head back home and make a stack of cash. Maybe get on TV, you know? I just never thought it would end up like it did."

I nodded. I never expected to fire my weapon in anger, never really expected to be in real danger. Never expected to have to kill to survive.

I couldn't think of anything to say. "Since when has life ever been straight forward?" It sounded hollow to me.

Kyle gave a good natured chuckle. "You're right, I guess." He sipped on his coffee, his attention momentarily distracted by a slim brunette walking by. He let out a low whistle, a wolfish smile on his face. "Now that was a sight I'm glad I survived for."

I turned, leaving Kyle to his leering. The company guys were unloading the baggage finally. Joe held up my bag, mouthing to me it was time to go.

"Time for you to go?" Kyle asked

"Yeah."

There's something I need to tell you, Mark. Before you go." He paused for a moment, as if struggling with his ability to find the right words. "When we first met I lied to you. Let me finish," he told me in a rush before I could reply. "I told you that I had contacts back home. The truth is that I don't. Nobody back home knows I'm here, I don't have the backing of a news channel. I sold my piece of shit car just to get enough money to get into Liberia. I saw a chance to report on something that was being ignored and I took it. I don't know what I'm going to do with all the footage but I know I've got something … unique. At the start, I just didn't want you to think I was a no-talent hack."

It wasn't an earth-shattering revelation. I always figured there was something he was holding back from me. I reached over, placing a hand on his shoulder. "Don't worry about it, Kyle. It's good of you to tell me."

"You're not mad?"

"No. I didn't give you a reason to be honest with me." I shrugged. "It's no big deal."

"Thanks, buddy." He pulled me in for a hug and I tried not to wince with the motion.

We moved apart. "I'd better get going, Kyle. The guys are waiting. Will you be alright?"

Kyle smiled again. "Of course. I get to sit on my ass and drink coffee for the rest of today. What's not to like?"

"Okay then. You take care, my friend." I stuck out a hand.

As we shook he said, "You should come to see me, once you're better and all. Would do you good."

I laughed. "I'll see what I can do. Good luck with the documentary, Kyle. And remember, don't put my face in the damn thing."

He laughed. I nodded to him a final time and turned. I wish that I had something worthwhile to say, something worthy of what we had been through, but I was beat up, tired and terrible at speeches. From behind, Kyle shouted, "Thank you, Mark."

I waved over my shoulder, too sore to turn, and not wanting to have to say another goodbye to him. As I hobbled toward Joe, I wondered what kind of documentary Kyle would make. How would he tell this story? At that moment, I was too tired to care.

Chapter Twenty-Five

I laid in a clean hospital bed, a private room to myself. The company rewarded their employees with the best medical care, even in France. It was a small private hospital in the suburbs of Paris. I stretched out, trying to ignore the two IVs linking my arm to a machine. One was in the back of my hand, the other in my forearm. Replacing lost fluids, I guessed. I had to buzz every twenty minutes or so for a nurse to come and hand me a bedpan. The pain plaguing me for so long in Liberia, and Guinea, had disappeared. It wasn't only fluids they pumped into me.

A knock at the door. It opened, and Joe stuck his head around. "You awake?"

"Sure, come on in, Joe."

Joe strode into the room, his mouth busily chewing gum. "Why the hell you lying in silence? There's a TV in the corner." Dressed in civvies – stonewashed jeans, and a red checked shirt – he looked strange. I was so used to seeing him geared up for combat. He dragged the padded seat over to my bedside. As had become habit, he touched my shoulder. "How you feeling?" He asked sitting down, still chewing.

"Can't feel much of anything. But that's a good thing." I pushed myself up the bed, mindful of the wires, so I was level with him. "I thought you'd be flying home today?"

He shook his head. "Can't head back until I know you're alright."

"Joe, I'm fine. You didn't have to do that. I'm fine."

"Uh huh. Clearly," he said looking me over. "That's why you're wired up, lying in hospital. Besides, staying in Paris works well for me. The food is out of this world."

I laughed, wiping at my eye.

"I spoke to your surgeon. It's good news. There's no permanent damage to your eye. The swelling will come down, you'll be able to open it in a few days. Your rib's broken, but I think you know that. They're treating the, uh, problem on your dick. Other than that, just dehydration and malnutrition. A week, maybe two, and you'll be discharged." He leaned closer, stopped chewing. "We also need to talk about what went on in Zorzor. Kyle told me some things, about Tiger King—"

"Tiger King?" My heart raced. "What did he say?"

"Just that he died, refusing to retreat with his men. Brave, but stupid."

Bless you, Kyle.

"I tell you," Joe continued, "not many people will miss him. Real bruiser. You know he wasn't even Liberian? No he was from Burkina Faso or somewhere. Just the lure of war brought him to LURD."

My heart just about returned to normal. Joe looked at me, his face scrunching in concentration. "If you'd rather write a report about what went on, that's fine. I know it must be difficult to speak about. Y'know what, make it a report when you're better. No hurry. Once you're home you can email it to me."

I'd always intended to deny knowledge of Tiger King's fate. Kyle had taken care of our cover story.

"That's good of you, Joe. Thanks." I stretched over, getting my plastic glass, and drank some water. "Thanks for allowing Kyle on the flight."

Joe shrugged as if it were no big deal.

"So what happens now?"

He let out a sigh, sitting back in his chair. He began chewing again. "We won't be going back to Liberia, that's for sure. Funding has been cut. Their rebellion is finished. Either way, it doesn't make much difference. There are always places to work. If this Iraq invasion goes ahead, we'll be in there. The government has already started sourcing out contractors. But I'm getting head of myself. For you, R and R. Get yourself back to health, and we'll talk."

I leaned back, letting the pillows take charge. I was fine not planning ahead. All I wanted to think about was getting better, healing my wounds, and getting back to work.

"I still feel bad, you know? Letting you head out to Zorzor on your own. I'd even thought of letting some of the other guys head out to other LURD strongholds. I just thank God I didn't, else we could've been dealing with deaths … well you know."

"Like I said, Joe. I wanted to go. It would have worked if the government hadn't made such sweeping advances. You did the right thing. They needed us spread out, not sitting in Voinjama."

"Hell, I guess so. It still doesn't make it any easier to swallow."

I stifled a yawn, hiding it with the back of my hand.

"You're tired," said Joe, starting to rise. "I should go."

The yawn came. "Sorry, it's the medication."

"I'll come back and check on you tomorrow, Mark. Just you concentrate on getting better, and we'll get you home."

"I'll do my best."

He left the room, closing the door behind with care. I stretched out, pulling my covers up to my chin. Closing my good eye, the image of the burning manor in Zorzor waited for me. My imagination filled in the sound effects. Screams and cries. Amongst it all, the sorrowful moans of the wounded child soldier I'd left to die. I'd read somewhere once that all veterans have one nightmare, an experience they carry from the field of battle to their dreams. The child soldier was my nightmare. He waited for me when I closed my eyes.

Chapter Twenty-Six

After five days in the French hospital, arriving home had been a sedate affair, like arriving at a funeral, something not enjoyed but something that had to be done. No fanfare waited for me, no crying relatives, no receptive well-wishers. Not that I expected any. Only a handful of people outside of the company knew where I had been and why. The less people that knew the better, it kept things simple. Awkward questions could be avoided though I expected many considering how long I'd been gone and how worn-down I looked.

Escaping the claustrophobic confines of Edinburgh's busy airport, a gray day, accompanied by a chilled rain, greeted me outside. I slid into a waiting taxi and watched the city slip by.

"Bit of bother at the weekend?" the driver asked.

"Something like that."

My answer, short and to the point, must have warned him off, as for the rest of the journey he remained quiet. We finally pulled up to the building. The car bounced the curb, jostling me in ways my body didn't appreciate. I ignored his apology, pushed a handful of notes through the space between the seats, and told him to keep the change. It didn't take the guy long to peel away after I slammed the door shut behind me.

I stared up at the old townhouse. For a while I didn't think I'd ever see this place again. Some years back it had been converted into separate flats. Mine resided on the second floor. I wasn't looking forward to climbing the stairs.

Standing alone in the quiet street, I was struck by how different it was being back home. Liberia was another world away and yet it was a world I felt more familiar with than this one.

I blew out a tired breath and used the unsteady handrail to help me up the six steps to the door. The rain fell heavier, almost a torrent but nothing like what I experienced while in the jungle. Slotting my key into the lock, I stepped inside, thankful to escape the drenching. The hall was dark, the only window high above the door never let in much light. A single light fixture hung from the entry, still without a bulb. Some things never changed it seemed. I ascended the stairs, each step creaked in turn. Behind, the faint scratch of the peephole cover moved. Mrs. Warrington doing her usual enthusiastic neighbourhood watch. I considered turning around, letting her see the condition I was in, give her something to chat about with her cronies. But I was too tired, too sore. I unlocked the last door, forcing it open against the resistance of mail piled behind it. I then gave it a sturdy kick, making sure it closed all the way. Dropping my bag, I retrieved the only package off the floor, cardboard encased in a layer of dark tape. I made my way through the flat, shivering at the sheer emptiness of the place. A heavy musk had descended in my absence. It was oppressive and smacked of solitude.

I reversed the package, and seeing Kyle's name on the back, tore into it. A fat packet of photographs fell into my lap with a hastily scrawled note taped to the front.

Mark. Here's all the photos from Liberia. Be warned, they're not edited. Thought you should have a copy of what I have. Will be in touch. Kyle.

There must have been a thousand or so, perhaps more. An unlabelled CD slid out alongside the pictures with 'Liberia' scribbled in black marker. The first few pictures I leafed through were shots Kyle must have taken before we met, possibly in Guiana. A dirt road, flanked by undergrowth. Nothing spectacular. Before I flipped to the next picture, something stopped me, as if some unseen force held my hand back. It was dread. I'd gone through so much to escape Liberia, I didn't want to go back, not even in pictures. I had enough images in my mind already, ones that I'd never forget. I threw the pictures and disc on the table. At some point I'd have to look at them, but. But not today. All I wanted to do for the next few days was sleep.

I stretched out, kicking my trainers off.

Kyle had been busy. What would he do with the footage? His problem, I told myself. But I knew it wasn't. Our fates were interlinked. What he chose to do with the footage would affect us both. How, it remained to be seen.

4251752R00082

Printed in Great Britain
by Amazon.co.uk, Ltd.,
Marston Gate.